EDITOR'S REVIEW

<u>What is love?</u>

I was immediately pulled into what was happening in *Whisper in the Night* even though I didn't completely understand what was going on. At first, I thought this was just another romance story. I was so wrong though. What happens in this book could never be classified as just normal romance. This has to be the most amazing love story ever written.

While reading and editing this book, I was taken on a roller-coaster ride of emotions. I cried with the characters, but I also smiled and laughed with them. This isn't one of those books that you read, put back on the shelf, and soon forget. The story of Marissa, Stephen, and Jason will take up residence in your memory, never to be forgotten.

Lisa Binion

Whisper in the Night

BOOK ONE OF THE
TANGLED HEARTS TRILOGY

S. S. MCLEISH

Published by KLAS Media Group. (**www.klasmediagroup.com**)

Whisper in the Night (Book one of the Tangled Hearts Trilogy).
Copyright © 2024 by S. S. McLeish.

ISBN 978-0-9847635-5-9 (paperback)
Romance, Women, Adult -Fiction

Edited by Lisa Binion
Book Layout by Shereece McLeish
Cover Design by GRB Media Group, LLC

TO LOVE...

ALWAYS,

S. S. MCLEISH

ACKNOWLEDGEMENTS

To my love and unwavering strength, Ryan; my fierce protector, Ajalon; and my mini bestie and cheerleader, Aryanna—your love fills my heart with joy.

A special thanks to Kerry, who embodies the essence of true friendship—a friend loves at all times.

To my family, my village, my tribe—your love and support are beyond measure.

To my Networking for Christ Ministry, (NFCM) church family, I am deeply grateful for your love and prayers.

My heartfelt appreciation goes to my wonderful editor, Lisa Binion, whose honesty and professionalism have been invaluable.

I am extremely grateful to Norje Media Films for their exceptional marketing, video production and photography skills.

A big thank you to Sequential Logic for their web hosting and technical support services.

Lastly, my gratitude to Maurice Gregory for his vocal mastery and production of *"Deja Vu"* song.

WHISPER IN THE NIGHT

Chapter 1

A gust of wind drags the discarded plastic bag along the battered dirt road, and the freshness of rain-kissed earth hangs enticingly in the air. Marissa kicks the empty juice box back and forth as it bounces off the fiberglass walls of the tiny phone booth.

The telephone presses between her ear and shoulder as she smiles and twirls her curly shoulder-length brown hair. She wipes away the remaining drops of rain that linger on her freckled arms and glances at the watch on her wrist.

"That's new," she thinks to herself. "I don't remember that one being there." She studies the newly identified freckle on the back of her hand.

"What's new?" the male voice on the other end of the line asks. Marissa realizes that she had wondered out loud, something she almost always does and usually at the most inopportune time.

"Ha ha, sorry, babe. Thinking out loud as usual." Her foot deftly feels around the phone booth for the juice box. She looks down and spots it in the far corner, too far away to reach it.

The male voice chuckles. "Still there?" he asks. "Issa, are you there?"

"Uh, yes. I'm still here. I found a new freckle. I don't think even you knew that one was there," she says teasingly.

"I know every single spot on you. I know their shapes; I know each path. Your freckles are an amazing artwork, divinely inspired, yes." He pauses then says with a husky voice, "I know them very well."

Marissa giggles, still twirling her hair.

"And right about now, I'm picturing your cheeks overflowing with color. Am I right?"

"Umm, no..." She giggles as her hand raises to touch her warm cheek. "Well maybe." Marissa peers through the foggy glass of the phone booth, trying to see the sky. "It's about to come down again. I'm gonna make a run for it. I'll call you when I get back to the hotel. Okay, babe?"

"Okay. Be safe." He sighs then says, "Issa, you're my whole heart. I love you and I miss you. Hurry home."

Tears sting the back of her eyes. She whispers, "I love you too, babe," then hangs up the phone. She dashes from the phone booth and is drenched by torrents of rain. She screams playfully as the downpour first hits her skin.

Through the deluge, she looks around for the sign that reads ATHENA STREET EAST and trods off in that direction. Her rugged boots make a splashing sound as they hit the dirt pathway, reminding her of earlier years when she and her younger sister would play in muddy puddles after a good dose of summer rain. She smiles at the good memory and makes a mental note to call her sister as soon as she gets back.

In the distance, the blue neon sign of HOTEL ATHENA is barely visible through the curtains of rain. She is fully drenched and her clothing clings to every inch of her. She takes a deep breath, filling her lungs with the earthy fragrance that permeates the air.

A car pulls alongside her and the door swings open. Marissa stares at the man and his kind smiling face. She hesitates as he motions to her and says, "Get in! Are you trying to catch your death of cold?"

"No, actually, I'm just trying to get back to my hotel."

"Let me guess, Hotel Athena?" he asks with a wry grin.

"Wow, how did you know?" Marissa asks sarcastically. On the remote island, Hotel Athena is the only hotel for miles. Marissa loves the seclusion of Hotel Athena. It was the perfect private haven to escape from the world.

"Come on. Get in then," he demands.

Marissa hesitates, but something about his face is intriguing and kind; his smile could stop the rain, or maybe, stop her heart. She gets in, still studying his smiling face.

"Tourist, huh? From what parts?" He watches briefly as she wipes the rain from her face with an already wet sleeve. "Here, try this." He hands her a towel. Their fingers touch for the briefest of moments. She looks at him. His gaze intense, he stares directly at her. She quickly looks away.

Marissa feels that familiar warmth creeping into her cheeks. She is grateful the car is dark, otherwise his effect on her would be seen all over her face. She touches her now flushed cheeks. Something about him connects with her. It's fleeting and exciting, and Marissa wants more.

Wait…Do I not know where I am from? Why am I acting like a teenager on her first date?

So?" he clears his throat, interrupting her thoughts. "Where are you from?"

"USA," she mutters, her breath caught in her throat. "Thanks for the towel." Her voice cracks. *Girl, what is wrong with you? Get it together! Oh, Lord! I hope I did not say that out loud. Breathe, Marissa, breathe.* She looks over at her rescuer. He is busy navigating his way back to the hotel. She relaxes; obviously, she didn't think out loud.

"USA? That's vague and a massive expanse of land if memory serves me right. Where in the US? Which of the *fifty* states are you from?" He looks questioningly at her.

Marissa laughs at his exaggerated tone and looks down at her fidgeting fingers. "That's all I'll say for now." She tosses the towel on the battered guitar case on the back seat. She studies him, curious to see if he is the musician type. "You play? What are you? Some kind of musician?"

His laugh is deep and throaty. "Yeah, some kinda. I've been known to dabble." He looks across at her. "What about you? What do you do?"

Marissa relaxes a bit more. "This and that." She smiles at the puzzled look on his face.

"You're just bursting with information, aren't you?" He smiles at her, sarcastically teasing. "USA. This and that. You're a shroud of mystery." He glances at her. "I'd like to tear away those guarded layers that you have up," he says in a very suggestive and flirtatious tone.

Marissa did not miss it. She smiles at him shyly then averts her gaze to the windshield wipers frantically doing their best to keep the windshield clear.

"There's no layers to me. What you see is what you get," she says, glancing back at him. He smiles intriguingly at her and again she looks away. "Anyway, enough about me. I detect an accent, but I can't place it."

From the corner of her eyes, she sees the HOTEL ATHENA sign drawing closer and closer. She doesn't want the conversation to end. *Could he be the one?* She shivers slightly and dismisses the thought as quickly as it came up.

She could not help but wonder though if her soaking wet clothes caused the chill or was it her thoughts of the handsome stranger just inches across from her? She tries to focus her mind elsewhere.

Her fingers follow the trail of a single raindrop making its way down the car window. He was silent, but Marissa feels like he is watching her. That excites her even more, but she dares not turn to look at him.

The car pulls slowly in front of the hotel. She feels a tiny bit disappointed that they are already there. He turns the car off and then looks at her, smiling broadly.

"Accent? Hmmm… What accent?" He takes her hand, still smiling.

Marissa looks at him puzzled. *Ahhh… yes, I did ask him about his accent,* she reminds herself.

The light from the hotel floods the car. *My God, he's gorgeous. OMG, that smile. Girl, you better not be talking out loud.* She grins uncomfortably at him. *Crisis averted. That was all in my head.*

"What's so funny?" he asks as he runs his thumb over the back of her hands. She quickly pulls away.

"Umm...nothing. Just something I remembered." She looks away from his intense stare.

"What's your name?"

She hesitates.

"Come on, at least give me that. I just rescued you from what is possibly the heaviest rainfall in the history of the world. More like a monsoon as a matter of fact. It hasn't rained this much since the days of Noah's flood. It was certain death."

"Wow, music and drama must have been your specialty in school," she teases. She watches him as he laughs. He has a great laugh. Marissa loves it.

He opens the car door and hands the keys to the valet who steps over. He motions to the other valet who is about to open Marissa's door. "I got it, thank you."

Marissa watches as he walks around the car to her door. He's tall, stately with rugged features, has a chocolate-mocha skin tone, and *mighty stars, is he handsome.* She drinks him all in.

He opens the door and stretches out his hand to her. For the briefest of moments, she hesitates but then takes his hand. She stands and he closes the door behind her then steps closer. Marissa steps back, her back now pressing against the car. He towers over her.

Her senses attempt to register the cologne he is wearing but her mind is racing too much for her to think.

"Tell me your name." His whisper is firm and demanding, and he is incredibly close.

Did I forget my name? She fumbles around in her muddled thoughts for the right thing to say. "Mari...Marissa," she stutters.

"See, that wasn't so hard, was it?" he says, hand outstretched. "Jason. Pleasure to make your acquaintance, ma'am." He grins at her and holds her gaze as he nods slightly like a proper English gentleman.

"Jason?" Marissa was slightly confused "Ohhh, yes, your name is Jason." Her cheeks flush with embarrassment, and she knows it is displayed all over her face. *Now is not the time to get all scatterbrained, Marissa!* She scolds herself. She tries to get past him, but he blocks her path.

"What's your hurry?" he laughs. "Gosh, you're shivering! Let's get you out of these clothes." Her T-shirt and jeans cling to every inch of her. Jason wonders if they are fitted or if it's because she's dripping wet. Either way, his eyes devour her.

Something about her quirky shyness, and the way she blushes intrigues him. He is drawn to her, yet he also feels very protective of her. He places his hand gently at the small of her back and leads her inside the lobby.

Marissa and Jason stand in the middle of the lobby staring at each other, oblivious of the other guests walking by. Neither is willing to go their separate ways. *Come back to earth, Marissa. Stop acting like a lovestruck teenage girl. You're twenty-nine for God's sake.*

"Well, umm...thank you for the ride. It was a pleasure meeting you." She stretches out her hand to Jason. He takes her hand and brings it slowly to his lips. Light and delicate as the touch of a butterfly, his lips brush across the back of her hand. She shivers again. *Nope, that's definitely not from being cold.*

He lingers over her hand. "The pleasure was purely mine." He studies her face as if examining every last freckle. She blushes, stirring uneasily. "You're as beautiful as your name, Marissa." Her name rolls off his tongue like a gentle caress. Marissa reluctantly pulls her hand away.

"Thank you. I better get out of these." She glances up into his hazel-brown eyes. *Gosh, he's such a beautiful man.* "I'm on the 10th floor." Marissa wasn't sure why she mentioned that, but at least she didn't include her room number.

"Yeah, you should get out of those. I'm on the12th." They walk toward the open elevator. Jason's and Marissa's fingers reach out at the same time to press the buttons to their floor. They exchange awkward smiles as the elevator door closes. The backs of their hands brush intentionally against each other's.

Jason wants to hold her hands, but he is uncertain if she would pull away from him. Finally he musters the courage and entwines his fingers with hers as they watch the numbers to each floor climb.

Marissa isn't sure when it happened, but she knows she is not dreaming. A million things run through her mind, a jumbled confused mess that refuses to settle on one particular thought or thing. *No, not confused, it's, it's...,* she can't quite put her finger on it, but this moment right here, right now, is real.

She pinches herself to ensure this is really happening. Jason's kiss is firm, seeking, demanding more of her. She clears her mind and gives in to the wave of emotions now cascading through her body.

Her lips part, giving him full access, and he gladly accepts. *Mighty stars, he is a good kisser.* An uncontrollable moan escapes her lips as Jason pulls her in even closer and deepens their kiss.

The throaty sound that escapes him, Marissa is not sure what it was, but she is confident he is enjoying the kiss as much as she is.

The elevator doors open, and a couple enters. The doors close. Marissa and Jason, still engulfed in a passionate kiss, are oblivious to the new occupants. A woman clears her throat as if to signal that Marissa and Jason are no longer alone.

Through the haze of passion, Marissa tries to pull away, but Jason's kiss is deliciously intoxicating. Her body is limp and helpless against him as his lips and tongue work masterfully over her lips, her face, her neck, then back to her lips.

He is an amazing kisser. Marissa's legs buckle beneath her, but Jason holds her steady against him. The evidence is screaming, pressing into her that he is as aroused as she is.

The elevator stops and Jason glances up at the floor number. He pulls Marissa toward the door, his lips never leaving hers as they exit. He backs her up against the wall next to the elevator, kissing her with a fierce growing hunger.

Reluctantly, they pull away from each other and walk a few doors down. Marissa, still dazed, surmises that she is on the 12th floor based on the numbering on the wall.

Jason fumbles for his key, his T-shirt now wet from where she was pressed up against him. Her cheeks flush when she remembers his lips on her in the elevator.

At last the door opens, and Jason holds it open for her to enter. She gives the room a quick once-over. Sheets of music are thrown across one of the beds in the room. A MacBook is open on the desk to a beach scene screensaver. A pair of jeans is flung over the chair, and a half-eaten slice of pizza is next to the computer.

Jason looks at her, his eyes asking as he reaches for her wet, snugly fitting T-shirt. "I should get you out of these," he says, staring intently at her.

"Yes, you should." She looks up at him. "After all, you do not want me to catch my death of cold," she nervously jokes, shocked at her air of confidence.

He smiles, pulling her closer and taking her shirt off in one fluid movement. Her wet shirt hits the carpeted floor, and her bra quickly follows. Jason steps back, his eyes roaming over her, drinking her all in. Marissa instinctively raises her hands to cover her breasts. Midway, he stops her.

"No, don't. Don't hide from me, Marissa." Her name was a whisper on his lips. "You're too exquisite to hide yourself."

Her face, hands, shoulders, and torso were covered with tiny freckles. Marissa had always been self-conscious about her freckles. That was, of course, before Stephen.

Marissa quickly pushes Stephen out of her mind. Jason steps closer and starts kissing her shoulders. "I love your freckles. They are divine."

Marissa froze. Her mind replays the phone conversation from earlier; Stephen also thinks her freckles are divine.

Jason senses her reaction in an instant. He stops, questioning what they are about to do. "We don't have to do this." He gently kisses the top of her head and lingers a bit, his nose taking a whiff of her hair. *Shea butter and coconut.* She smells delicious, she tastes delicious, and he is content with simply kissing her all night.

He can hear his lips reassuring her that they can stop, even though his mind and loins are definitely screaming something else. "We can talk, or I can take you…"

His voice trails off as Marissa touches his face. Her fingers graze over the slight stubble of hair. He must have shaved this morning, she notes to herself. The slight beard on his face is still sharp to the touch. Her fingers trace his lips, and he gently nips at them. She shudders as his tongue draws a circle around her finger.

She gazes up at him then tiptoes to plant a kiss on his lips. She takes his hand and places it on her belly, just above the clasp of her jeans. She hears herself saying, "I don't want you to stop." *You're all kinds of confident today*, she thought to herself.

He looks down at her. Her face is flushed, and her lips look soft and inviting. He wants her, and he is sure she wants him just as much, yet he hears himself asking, "Are you sure?" His eyes search her face, "Because we don't have to. Being with you this way is enough."

Marissa's response is to tug upward on his damp shirt. He helps her pull his shirt over his head, and it joins her bra and shirt on the carpet.

They stand there for what seems like eternity gazing at each other. Her hand reaches up and touches his rippled chest, and for a fraction of a second, he trembles. His eyes are ablaze, full of passion for her. Her hands trail a path across his chest, and soon, her lips follow.

His reaction to the mere touch of her hands surprises him, and he wonders what she is doing to him. *Keep it together, dude*, he warns himself. Yet he can't help biting his lips as Marissa's hands inch lower and lower still.

Her hand pauses at the scar on his abdomen, her fingers gently tracing the path of his scar. Her mouth dry, she can barely speak. "What happened?" she asks.

"Long story," he replies, his tongue moistening is now dry lips.

She gazes up at him as her hands open his belt uckle then pull at the clasp of his jeans. He does the ame and starts pushing the wet jeans down over her ips. He steps back and watches as she steps out of hem.

Now she stands before him in nothing but her nderwear. Instinct sets in, and again, she attempts to over up, but Jason reaches for her hands. He wags his inger, smiling at her, and brings her hands to his lips. Ie kisses the tip of each finger.

"Marissa, my delicate flower, don't hide ourself from me. I wanna explore every inch of you."

Marissa trembles at the thought of him xploring every inch of her. If his exploration is nything like his lips on hers, Marissa knew she was in or a treat.

He scoops her up, walks over to the bed, and ays her gently on it. His eyes never leave hers as he nzips his pants and pulls them all the way off. He is bulging beneath his underpants, straining to get out.

He lifts one of her feet to his lips and kisses her toes, then his tongue glides up to her ankle. Marissa had no clue that life existed there until now. She bites her lips to prevent herself from screaming.

"Ohhh, that feels good," she breathes out loud. His tongue is now at the back of her knees and slowly charting a path upward. Marissa's hands clench the sheet as his lips caress the very essence of her. *This is really happening.* Moans escape her as Jason's tongue masterfully dances along her inner thighs.

Her mind again thinks of Stephen, but he is shoved away as Jason's tongue caresses her innermost.

"Let me look at you." Jason's eyes are alive with passion. "I want you."

Marissa reaches for him. "I want you too."

Their kiss is full of deep passionate longing as their hungry lips devour each other. His eyes look like shimmering flames as they lock with hers. Moans of pleasure escape them both as Jason enters her.

Marissa's fingers caress Jason's back as her body adjusts to the width of him. He can feel her tightening around him, but he bites his lip, willing himself to hold it together.

Contrasting slick brown skins slide against each other as they move in oneness until they reach the pinnacle of their pleasure.

Their trembling bodies, entwined in silken sheets, collapse against each other. Marissa feels like she has exploded into a million little happy pieces.

She tries to blink away the tears at the back of her eyes, but they roll down her cheeks. He kisses her freckled shoulders, then looks at her.

"Did I hurt you?" he asks, his voice husky and his eyes still ablaze with the pleasure of her.

"No," she whispers, still trembling as he kisses away her tears. "Quite the opposite," she says, smiling through her tears.

She feels his desire growing once more. He bites at her lips, his tongue demanding entrance. Soon the flame ignites. Sometime later, much later, their bodies urgently race toward a mind-blowing abyss. Marissa whispers his name as her body becomes undone. Unable to hold back the rising flood within, he lets go and allows the waves to wash over him.

He kisses her softly and pulls her closer to him. He feels her lips on his neck as her body relaxes against his body. The last thing he remembers is the delicious smell of coconut and shea butter as he kisses the top of her head and then falls asleep.

Through the half-drawn curtains, the night sky is visible. The rain clouds have parted, and tiny stars sprinkle the sky.

Marissa gazes at him as he sleeps. He is gorgeous. She could lie in his arms forever. She breathes him in, making a mental note of the way he looks, the way he smells.

She kisses the lips that just brought her exquisite, unexplainable, mind-altering pleasure, then she too drifts off to sleep.

Chapter 2

Sunlight streaming through the window onto her, Marissa opens her eyes. Jason is still fast asleep beside her, his arms wrapped around her. She gently eases out of his embrace, slowly inching off the bed, and dresses quietly.

She stares at his body barely covered by the sheet; in the heights of their passion, she did not notice that the scar on his hip ran all the way to his side. *What happened to mar such beauty?*

Jason stirs, and Marissa quickly scribbles on a notepad on the nightstand next to the bed. She looks one last time at perfection lying in the bed, fighting the temptation to lift the covers and crawl back beneath the sheets with him.

It takes all of her strength not to wake him and repeat last night's magic all over again, but she knows better. She knows exactly what this is. Now is the time for her to exit.

Every inch of her body replays last night's scenes. She still tastes him on her lips. She wishes that what they experienced could last.

She wants to know more about this man who brought her soul to life but shrugs off the sadness that threatens to creep in.

She kisses her fingers and gently places them on his lips. Smiling, she quietly exits.

A few moments later, Jason yawns and stretches. His hand reaches over and blindly searches the other side of the bed. He sits up and looks around.

"Marissa?" He gets up and heads to the bathroom. "Marissa?" He walks back and sits on the bed. *Was last night a dream*? He knows it wasn't; her scent still fills the sheet and engulfs the room.

He glances over at the nightstand and reaches for the note. It reads: FOREVER IN MY HEART. XOXO! MARISSA.

Jason lies back on the bed and looks up at the ceiling. He reads the note again and smiles. "Mysterious Marissa." The smile quickly fades from his face the moment he realizes that he does not know her last name or how to even begin to find her.

He looks at the back of the note and finds it blank. No telephone number, and nothing to go on but her first name.

"Tenth floor, that's where she said she was." He picks up the phone and dials guest services. "Well, hello there. I'm Jason Saunders in 1218. Can you connect me to Marissa on the 10th floor?"

Jason knows it is a long shot, but he has to try. He listens intently to the voice on the other end of the phone, "No, I don't know the exact room number." He listens again, "No, I don't know her last name either. Yes, I know, but this is an emergency." Jason places his head in his palm. "Okay, thank you for trying. Have a good day too."

He hangs up the phone, lies back on the bed, and stares at the ceiling. He eyes the thin crack in a part of the ceiling. *What did you expect though, dude? Did you think they'd just give you her info?*

Memories of Marissa's freckled brown skin, intoxicating smell, and shy smile floods his mind. He has to get out. His body is already betraying him at the very thought of her. He dresses quickly, grabs a beach towel, and heads out the door.

Jason's eyes roam over the already crowded beach, searching each cabana. He looks at each scantily clad female, hoping to find a certain freckled temptress.

"Can I get you a drink, Mr. Saunders?" Jason turns to see Julio, a bartender at Hotel Athena.

"Julio, my man," Jason says, "do you happen to know a guest on the 10th floor, beautiful brown skin, cutest freckles, brown hair, just simply beautiful? You can't miss her."

Julio stares at Jason, "She sounds beautiful, but no, I don't know her."

Jason holds his head. "Is there anyone you could ask to do me a favor by getting me her room number or her last name?"

Julio stares at Jason as if he's crazy. "So, Mr. Saunders, do you want that drink?" Julio's expression tells Jason that he doesn't stand a chance with him.

"I'm sorry, man," Jason says. "I shouldn't have asked that of you. Thank you, but no, I'm gonna pass on that drink." Jason pats Julio on the shoulders, places a few loose bills on his tray, and walks off. As he enters the lobby, he remembers the valet from the night before. He runs out toward the valet counter.

"Mr. Saunders, do you need your car?" the valet asks.

Jason looks at his nametag and sees the guy's name is Andres.

Andres, no, I don't need my car, but I was wondering...." he pauses and thinks for a second before he continues, "the girl I was with last night, petite, beautiful, curly brown hair, freckles." He looks at Andres, wondering if he was understanding him. "Have you seen her?"

"Ah, yes, Miss Marissa, yes, very beautiful." Andres smiles broadly. Jason glares at him. "No, I mean yes, I have seen her. She left earlier this morning."

"Left as in gone or left as in will return to the hotel later?" Jason asked hopefully.

"No, definitely left as in gone. She had her suitcase."

"Did you happen to get her last name?"

Andres looks at Jason puzzled, then finally responds. "No, I don't know her last name."

Jason thanks Andres and walks back to the lobby. As he enters the elevator, he remembers how small and fragile Marissa felt against his frame.

He dreads going back to his room, knowing her presence will still be lingering there. He has no appetite to eat, so breakfast is not an option.

As he enters the room, his mind replays last night. He could almost hear her moans of pleasure and how she felt against him. He replays their brief conversation in his mind, trying to find a clue.

He looks over at the rumpled sheets and remembers her girlish giggles as they got caught in them. Jason knows that he needs to focus on something else.

He takes up his computer and opens the screen to a blank page. He types in bold letters: WHISPER IN THE NIGHT.

***

Marissa stares out at the blue sky barely littered with clouds. She smiles and closes her eyes as memories of last night's lovemaking flash across her mind.

She looks out at the ocean below and thinks of the tiny island escape that she was on earlier. Her hand moves to her belly, and she rubs it gently. She can still hear Jason's seductive whispers during their lovemaking.

She has not felt this alive in a long time. All her long dormant senses now heightened; Marissa bites her lip as she thinks about him gently exploring every trembling inch of her body.

Overhead, the pilot announces that they will be landing soon. She is now back on US soil. Jason and that mesmerizing smile of his is now distant, yet the presence of him still lingers.

She wishes that she knew about more about him or even his last name, but again she reminds herself that it was one night. That is all it could be.

Now in a taxi, the familiarity of her city is a welcoming distraction as she watches the expanse of the skyline, littered with artistically designed buildings, swiftly drift out of sight.

Did he think of me when he woke up? Is he thinking of me now? Everything in her tells her that she affected Jason as much as he did her, that their connection was real.

She drags herself from the land of what-ifs. She knows what it was, and it makes no sense to dwell on things that cannot happen. The taxi pulls in her driveway. She thanks the driver and exits.

Marissa drags her suitcase along the stone pathway to her front door. The mailbox on the wall beside the green front door is brimming over with neglected mail. She grabs the unopened mail and browses through the lot.

She takes a deep breath as she turns her key in the door. Placing her suitcase to the side, she takes off her coat and hangs it in the closet.

"Babe, are you here?" a voice calls out.

"I'm in here, darling." Marissa turns, excited, and heads toward the kitchen.

The fridge door closes, and Stephen wheels toward Marissa. He smiles at her. She reaches down and kisses him then sits on his lap and kisses him passionately. Stephen's long arms encircle her.

"Someone missed me," Stephen says between Marissa's kisses.

Marissa holds Stephen's face and stares into his brown eyes. She kisses his lips gently then runs her finger through his thinning blond hair. "Of course I missed you, silly." She kisses him again, "Very much as a matter of fact."

"So I didn't hear back from you last night. Does that mean it happened?" Stephen asks.

Marissa gets up and walks toward the fridge. She circles a date in bright red on the magnetic calendar on the fridge door. She opens the fridge and gets a bottle of water, taking a drink before looking at Stephen. His face is a mixture of hope and sadness.

"Yes, it happened." She walks over and touches his face. "Yes, it did." She's now looking in his eyes, his head tilted toward her. "But are you okay, babe? I mean...are you still good with this?"

"It's too late now for that, isn't it?" Stephen says sadly.

"Babe...huh?" Marissa holds her head. "Babe, you wanted this… we discussed this…" Her eyes well with tears.

"But now that it has actually happened, I have to live with it. I cannot undo it!"

Her voice grows louder. "I wanted to adopt! You said the baby needs to be a part of one of us! You decided that, Stephen! You did! I was fine with adopting or being artificially inseminated! You, Stephen Paisley, said you didn't want that for me! I did not coerce you, and I sure did not hold a gun to your head! You decided this! Now own up to it and be a man about it! Don't come to me now with this bull after the deed you wanted done got done!"

"Yes, I said it! I decided!" Stephen quips angrily.

Marissa, crying hysterically, runs from the room. She collapses on the sofa in the living room as she sobs uncontrollably.

Stephen wheels up to the sofa. He reaches for her and pulls her onto his lap. He holds her face and kisses her tears. "I'm sorry, darling. You know you are my whole heart. I am not trying to hurt you. You know that, right?" He kisses her lips. "Issa, you know this, right?"

She nods and glances at him through her tears.

"Issa, I am thirty-seven, and I can't give my wife what we most want...a baby, our baby. That hurts me, honey. Iraq stole that from me, from us."

"Babe, I have what I most want...you. When will you see that?" Marissa asks, kissing Stephen. "I know… I know what Iraq stole from you...from us...but you got me, you got us, and hopefully in a few months, a little version of us will be running around."

Stephen places his hand on her belly. "Hopefully," he says, kissing her again. "So who was he? How was he? Was he gentle? Did he hurt you? Are you okay?

Marissa looks away, "I don't know his name. Honey, we promised not to talk about this. We'll see in a few weeks. What would you like for dinner?"

Marissa hurries off Stephen's lap. She's afraid her face will betray her. *Yes, I know his name,* her mind screams. *I know how his lips felt against my skin. I know his touch, his taste, I know him all too well.*

The realization dawns on Marissa that Jason was more than one night. She realizes that she will never forget him. His imprint will last a lifetime.

Stephen looks up at Marissa, sadness in his eyes. He rubs his amputated limbs. "I'm fine with anything you make, Issa." Stephen wheels from the room. "Goddamn Iraq," he mutters as he exits in haste. As soon as he exits the room, he buries his face in his hands and cries.

His mind replays the day in Iraq that forever changed his life. Stephen's unit was out patrolling. The sun was high in the sky, and the dust was thick and hung in the air. Out of the corner of his eyes, Stephen saw a little girl coming toward them. Her raven black hair was almost more than her tiny frame. He reached into his uniform pocket and pulled out a piece of candy like he always did. It wasn't until the little girl got closer that he noticed the bomb strapped to her back.

Stephen worked frantically to get the bomb off the now frightened girl, and a young private ran over to him to help get the vest off her. It took an eternity to get the vest off. As the private grabbed hold of the vest, Stephen noticed the timer counting down with only four seconds remaining.

Not having much time to think, Stephen grabbed the vest just as it detonated. His body became a human shield for the private and the little girl, preventing them from being blown to shreds.

In saving their lives, Stephen lost so much more. The little girl with the raven black hair and the young private still haunt Stephen's dreams ever so often. Their faces are forever etched in his memory.

He has replayed that day countless times in his head, tried to come up with different scenarios, but all led back to him taking the same path even if it cost him everything.

***

Marissa tosses the food around on her plate. She looks across the table at Stephen, who has barely touched his food. "Babe, you love my baked fish. You've barely touched it."

Stephen looks down at the food then back at Marissa. "I don't have much of an appetite today." He stares at her intently. "I've got too much on my mind." Marissa gets up from the table and removes their plates. Stephen listens as utensils clang together angrily.

Marissa reenters the room and removes the glasses from the table. Stephen holds onto her hand as she passes. "Issa, you're upset with me. I can tell."

Marissa glares at him. "Upset? I am not upset! I am angry!" She tries to pull away, but Stephen holds firm to her hand.

"I'm sorry, Issa. It's just that..."

Marissa cuts him off. "You're sorry?" Marissa rolls her eyes. "That's the understatement of the year. I am the one that is sorry. I am sorry I listened to you. I'm sorry I trusted you. I'm sorry I believed that we..." Marissa points to herself and Stephen, "...were in this thing together. How stupid of me." Marissa yanks her hand away. "I'm going to bed. Last night was a very, very long night," she says.

Stephen wheels away from Marissa. She watches as he disappears down the hall. She knows she hurt him and wishes she could take it back.

"Stephen! Babe, I'm sorry. Babe..." Marissa catches up with Stephen and kneels before him on the ceramic tile. It's extremely hard and cold under her knees. Marissa grits her teeth and bears the pain. Stephen's hurt and she's the cause. "Stephen, I'm sorry. I didn't mean it. Babe, listen to me, I'm so sorry." Stephen looks at Marissa as she pleads, "Come to bed, babe."

Stephen pulls back from Marissa and wheels around her. "Issa, you're my whole heart. You know this, honey. Right now though, I just want to be alone. I'll sleep in the guest room tonight." Stephen wheels away.

"Stephen, Stephen, babe, stop, please." Marissa calls after him, "This isn't like us, babe. Come on. Let's talk. We can't go to bed like this."

Stephen continues down the hallway while Marissa stands there gazing after him, tears streaming down her face. She searches her mind for anything that will make her feel better. There is nothing. This is one big mess that she knows cannot be undone.

Upstairs in their bedroom hours later, Marissa tosses and turns. Her fight with Stephen is at the forefront of her mind, yet she can't help but remember Jason's sweat-slicked skin moving rhythmically against hers. She hasn't felt alive like she did with Jason in years.

She gazes at the photograph of her and Stephen hanging on the wall. It was their wedding day.

Marissa's mind flashes back to their wild and passionate wedding night. She chuckles at the memory of Stephen completely spent from their passionate lovemaking.

He had joked that he had never worked so hard for anything in his life, and that it took a one-carat diamond ring to finally get her into his bed.

A twinge of sadness creeps in. Stephen had been fully whole. He had carried her to their honeymoon suite and made love to her over and over and over again until they were both exhausted. They lay there motionless as Stephen whispered to Marissa, "All I want is you, Issa. You're my whole heart."

They spent a week in honeymoon bliss, laughing, dancing, making love, and then making love again, completely emptying themselves with each other. Shortly after that, Stephen was deployed. That was eight years ago.

They had not shared that kind of intimacy since then. They had tried on several occasions, but it always ended with Stephen being angry at all that he had lost. Not only had he lost limbs, but the very definition of what made him a man was also stolen.

Even though Stephen bore the physical scars, she had also lost just as much.

Last night with Jason reminded her that she was still a woman, raging with raw passion and desire. The side of her that had been asleep for so long came alive and free in his arms.

Now that it's awake, Marissa is not sure she can dismiss it or tame it. Tears stream down the side of her face and soak through her pillowcase. *Gosh, how did things get so complicated?*

Somewhere between enchanting memories and tears, Marissa drifts off to sleep.

Meanwhile, Stephen sits in a chair in the guest bedroom, a glass of brown liquor in his hands. He downs it in one gulp, pours another, and downs that one too.

He looks over and remembers making love to Marissa on the hardwood dresser in the corner. They were young and free then, and their whole life was ahead of them.

He remembers making love to Marissa in every room of their newly bought home. Shortly after, he was deployed, and their lives forever changed.

He sees himself in the mirror. Disgust registers on his face. He throws the glass at the mirror and smashes it. In that moment, Stephen wishes that he had died in the blast. Marissa would be free, and he would not feel this helpless nothingness that plagues his daily thoughts.

Resignedly, he pulls himself into bed, hoping that he drank enough to put him to sleep, and that tomorrow would be a much better day.

***

Sunlight streams through the half-open blinds. Marissa wakes to the smell of bacon.

Still groggy, her eyes focus on the portrait of her and Stephen on the wall. This one was taken a few days after their wedding, and a couple at the hotel they were staying at snapped a picture of Stephen carrying Marissa toward the water. Marissa smiles at the happy memory.

Remembering last night's argument, she buries her face in her pillow and lets out a loud groan. "Get up, Marissa! Put on your big girl panties and go fix your marriage." She gets up and stretches, "Gosh, I'm beginning to sound like my mother. Ugh!" Marissa shudders at the thought.

She walks into the kitchen wearing one of Stephen's jerseys. Stephen is in the process of placing strawberries on the table. His eyes devour her as she enters.

Score! she thought. Stephen has never been able to resist the sight of her in his jersey, no matter how mad at her he was. She walks over and kisses the top of his head. "Good morning, babe. It sure smells good in here."

Stephen reaches up, holds her face, and kisses her on the lips. Marissa kisses him back, relaxing into his kiss. Reluctantly, she pulls away. She looks at him, uncertainty evident on her face.

"What's that for?" she asks.

Between kisses, Stephen replies, "That's a your husband has been a fool. I messed up. How do I fix it? Apology kind of kiss." He kisses her again.

Marissa pulls away.

"I'm trying to say I'm sorry," Stephen continues. "You're right. This was my idea, and when you did it, I made you feel like a... like a..." Stephen searches for a word.

"Like a whore?" Marissa says through gritted teeth.

"Issa, no, not like that." Stephen looks down at his hands then back at her. "I'm sorry I made you feel that way. The fact is, Issa, I panicked. You know you are my whole heart. Hurting you is like hurting myself. Honey, please say you forgive me," Stephen begs. "If you are pregnant…" Stephen pauses. "Actually, no, if we are pregnant, I'm looking forward to being his or her or both," he grins at her. "Issa, I'm looking forward to being a dad, to sharing this experience all with you."

Marissa's heart melts. "This will be our experience, Issa. I will be with you all the way. Come on. Say you forgive me, please," Stephen urges.

"Do your famous biscuits come with that bacon?" Marissa asks.

"Yes, ma'am. I'm just about to pull them from the oven."

"Then you're forgiven." Marissa grins, kissing Stephen. He pulls her down on his lap and kisses her deeply. His kiss is forceful, a mixture of willpower, hope, and desperation.

Stephen so wants to be the man he once was for Marissa. He remembers occasions of Marissa sprawled across the table wearing nothing but his jersey. Oh, how he wishes he could recapture those days.

The oven bell goes off, signaling that the biscuits are ready. Stephen agonizingly pulls his lips away from Marissa. He clears his throat. "Umm, I better get those." His voice is hoarse and raspy.

"Yes, yes you should," says Marissa, still kissing him. "Yes, you really should." Stephen tightens his hands around her waist and pulls her all the way into him. Her breasts crush against his chest.

"Now? I should get them now?" he asks between kisses.

"Hmmm," Marissa lets out a moan as she leans into him and kisses him deeper. In the background, the oven bell continues. Marissa and Stephen are lost in the taste of each other. Marissa hopes the moment will last, but she can already feel Stephen pulling away.

"Hmm...honey...I'm sorry...I'm sorry...I can't." As quickly as it started, the moment ends, leaving Marissa once again disappointed and wanting more.

Stephen pulls the golden biscuits from the oven and places them on the counter. He avoids Marissa's eyes as he moves across the kitchen.

Marissa says grace; they sit and eat in silence.

Chapter 3

Marissa races from the bed and heads to the bathroom. Stephen wakes up to the sound of retching.

The toilet flushes then there is the sound of water running. Stephen stretches and yawns.

It's been a few weeks since their last big fight, and things are still a bit tense between them. "Are you okay, babe?" Stephen pulls himself up in bed. "Issa, are you okay, honey?"

Inside the bathroom, Marissa stares at herself in the mirror. "It will be okay," she tells herself.

Stephen calls out again. "Issa, you're scaring me."

Marissa appears in the bedroom, her skin pale and flush. "I'm fine." She looks down at the blue-and-white test in her hand then hands it to Stephen.

He stares at it for what seems like eternity. He looks up at Marissa then back at the test.

"We're pregnant?" he asks with excitement, a big grin on his face.

Marissa lets out a big sigh of relief and plops down on the bed beside him. Stephen pulls her to him.

"You're pregnant!" Stephen laughs aloud, hugging Marissa tightly.

"No, babe, you got it right the first time. We are pregnant!"

Stephen hugs Marissa to him and kisses her neck. He buries her head on his chest then his smile fades and sadness registers in his eyes.

Marissa looks up at him. "Are you happy, babe? Are you okay?"

Stephen hesitates for a bit. He holds her face and kisses her on the forehead. "I'm happy. We both wanted this." He kisses her again, "I love you so much. You are my whole heart." He lets out a roar of laughter that takes Marissa by surprise. "I'm going to be a daddy! Now that's hilarious."

Marissa looks at Stephen's face. He hasn't laughed like that in ages. "What's hilarious about that?" Marissa laughs at Stephen. "You're gonna be a great dad."

Stephen laughs even harder. He tickles Marissa playfully adding, "You're gonna be a hot mama."

Marissa kisses him on the lips. "Let's hope you say that when my belly starts pushing you off this bed in a few months."

Stephen rubs Marissa's belly. He kisses her. "We are going to be parents, Issa, with a real human baby."

Marissa laughs, "I hope it will be a human baby."

"So what do we do now?" Stephen asked. "Do we get a crib? Oh, I will ask dad to come over and install a stair gate. I can start on the other childproofing."

Marissa looks at Stephen, laughing. "Slow down, Daddy. We are nowhere near there yet."

Relief washes over Marissa. She is happy that Stephen is happy. She kisses him. "That's way down the road. First, I have to call my doctor to see if she can see us today. Then I have to call Mom and Jade because..." Marissa grimaces at the thought of calling her mom. She has avoided calling her mom since she returned from her trip.

Stephen touches her face reassuringly. "Your mom will be fine, and even if she's not," he turns her face so that he's staring her dead in the eyes, "even if she's not, this is about us and no one else. You're happy, right?" Marissa nods. "Then that's all that matters to me, you and our baby."

Stephen realizes that he actually likes the sound of "our baby" very much. He pulls Marissa closer. "Our baby...do you hear how nice that sounds?" He hugs her. "Let's just lie here for a minute before we start letting the world in. I don't want this moment to end."

Marissa hugs him close, whispering, "We are gonna be parents."

***

Dr. Bland's office is decorated with images of pregnant moms of all shapes, shades, and sizes. Marissa studies each canvas, wondering what each mother was thinking at that moment.

Excitement stirs inside of her about the life growing within. She looks over at Stephen; he seems genuinely happy. She loves Stephen. She would be heartbroken if he were not happy.

She thinks of Jason. If she is being honest with herself, she thinks about Jason every day. This life within her is also his. *Is he doing okay*? *Have I crossed his mind since that night*?

For the briefest of moments, Marissa thinks of what it would be like with Jason if her life were different. She envisions his beautiful eyes lighting up when she tells him she's pregnant. She imagines handing Jason a pregnancy test. He studies it intently then lifts Marissa off the ground. He twirls her around and kisses her passionately. He kneels and kisses her belly. "I love you, beautiful Marissa. I can't wait to meet our child."

"I love you too, honey."

Jason kisses her passionately then lifts her and gently lays her on the bed and starts kissing a trail down her neck.

Marissa snaps back to reality. *Get your head straight, Marissa.* She forces herself back to the present.

"Why do you need to get your head straight?" Stephen asks, curious.

Marissa's face brightens; she had spoken out loud. She fumbles to find an answer for Stephen. "I was just thinking what my mom may say when we tell her we're pregnant."

Stephen looks at Marissa, puzzled. "You spoke to her when I was in the shower this morning, no?" He studies her face.

Marissa prays her face is not lying even though her lips are. "No, that was Jade. Umm, Mom was asleep. It's okay though." She went on, "This way when I speak with her later, I will have more details for her."

Stephen nods. "So, what did Jade say?" he asks.

Marissa wants to stop talking before her mouth betrays her. Just then, Dr. Bland walks in. She is a short stocky woman from West Africa who never ceases to remind her patients how blessed they are to give birth in such stellar conditions.

"So, Marissa, Stephen, my two favorite people, so what do I owe this pleasure?" Dr. Bland's accent is thick and rich. She walks over to Stephen and hugs him and then Marissa. Stephen and Marissa grin at her.

Dr. Bland walks toward the chart holder and picks up the result from Marissa's urine test that her nurse placed there earlier then adjusts her glasses on her face.

She looks up at a grinning Marissa and Stephen and smiles back at them. "I can confirm that you're pregnant!"

Dr. Bland takes up her calendar, "From my calculation you're just around four to five weeks pregnant. About the size of a poppy seed. A spring baby! That's exciting! Let me just check to make sure everything else is good. So, who wants to hop into the examining chair? Do you wanna go, Stephen?" Dr. Bland teases.

"I guess that would be me and our little poppy seed hopping in," Marissa says as they all laugh.

Stephen and Marissa hold each other's hands, grinning from ear to ear as Dr. Bland outlines their due date and what they should expect over the coming months. Stephen kisses Marissa's hand as he listens.

"I can't wait to meet him or her." Dr. Bland looks at both of them, smiling. "I know you both have been waiting for this moment for a long time. There's no one else more deserving than you two. When the time comes, do you want to know what you're having?"

"A human we hope and not a poppy seed," Stephen says, laughing. Marissa and Stephen look at each other, smiling, and then Stephen responds, "Yes, Dr. Bland, we would like to know."

Dr. Bland congratulates them as they leave her office beaming with pure joy.

***

Marissa and Stephen's Ford Explorer pull into his parents' driveway. His mom, Cathryn, greets them at the car before the engine is even turned off.

"Marissa, oh honey, look at you. You're practically glowing." She hugs Marissa through the window.

"Mom, give her a chance to get out of the car," Stephen laughs.

"Oh, yes, sorry. I don't want to hurt my grandbaby," Cathryn says.

"It's fine, Cathy. Oh, how I've missed you," Marissa says, stepping out of the Explorer and giving her mother-in-law a tight hug.

Cathy's short stocky frame clings to Marissa. She is a big hugger, and Marissa lives for those hugs. Her silvery blonde hair smells of a mixture of spices and some other product that Marissa can't quite put her finger on.

"What can I get you?" Cathryn asks, still excited. "I made your favorite pasta. I also made the pecan pie that you love, and there is honey garlic chicken. Oh wait, that might be too spicy for my granddaughter. I'll make another type of chicken, maybe baked. What would you like?" Cathryn rambles on while Marissa laughs.

"Mom, you have to slow down. I doubt Issa can eat all of that," Stephen says.

"Oh, hush, Stevie. She's eating for two. Of course she can eat that," Cathryn says, dismissing Stephen as she helps him from the car.

Stephen's dad, Nathan, now at the door, towers over his wife. A silvery gray beard covers his strong jawline.

"Woman, are you gonna allow them to come in?" he asks, laughing at Cathryn. He kisses Marissa's cheeks and hugs his son. "She's been running around here since you called this morning, Stevie. I think she cooked everything that was in the house." Stephen laughs at his dad.

"Don't worry. I'm sure you and I can handle the burden." Stephen replies.

"You bet, son, especially the pecan pie," Nathan laughs."

"Nathan Paisley, if you know what is good for you, you won't dare look at that pecan pie. It's for my granddaughter. I told you that already." Cathryn laughs, whacking Nathan on the hand.

"I already told you it's a grandson. Just you wait and see." Nathan tickles Cathryn as she passes by him.

Marissa smiles at the playfulness of her in-laws. Even after forty years of marriage they are still evidently in love with each other. From the moment she met the Paisleys, she wanted hers and Stephen's love story to be like theirs.

Inside the Paisley's house, it is quaint and homey. A collage of pictures of Stephen ranging from birth to high school, his wedding, and his time in the army decorate the wall.

On a side table are trophies and awards, all bearing Stephen's name. Marissa loves coming here and always feels quite at home.

The aroma of pie and spices lingers in the air. Much later a satisfied Marissa sets her fork down on her now empty plate, a contented smile on her face. "I think I ate way too much," she says to Stephen, rubbing her stomach.

"Yes, I think you did. You were shoveling down that pecan pie. I think you're taking this eating for two thing literally." Stephen laughs at Marissa's shocked expression.

"Stephen Paisley! I can't believe you said that!" Marissa says, laughing. "Soon you'll be calling me fat."

"Never," he says, leaning over to kiss her.

Cathryn and Nathan watch the exchange between Marissa and Stephen. "It's great to see you both so happy. You deserve all the happiness in the world," Cathryn says, hugging her son.

Nathan reaches over and rubs Marissa's hand. "I can't wait to meet my granddaughter," Cathryn says.

"Grandson," Nathan chimes in just as Cathryn slaps him on the hand playfully.

***

Back inside the car, Stephen smiles at Marissa as they drive to her parents' house. "Try to relax, Issa. I can see the tension by the way you're gripping the steering wheel."

He rubs her legs reassuringly. "It will be okay. Your mom will be happy for us."

"I hear you, babe, but I know my mom, and we both know she's not Cathy." Marissa laughs at Stephen's expression. "Like you said, this is about us and no one else. So I'll be fine whether she's happy or not. Lord, help me to be patient," Marissa prays. Stephen lets out a throaty laugh.

The car pulls into her parents' driveway. Jade is at the door as Marissa rings the bell. "Get in here, preggers!" Jade says, hugging her sister.

"Shhh!" Marissa whispers, "Does Mom know already?"

"No," Jade grins. "I'mma leave that to you," she winks, "but I did tell Dad. He's a softy, probably still crying."

"No, I'm not!" Graham, Marissa's stepdad, appears in the living room, "Come here, Peanut," he says, arms wide-open, waiting to hug Marissa.

"Hi, Daddy," Marissa says, falling into her father's arms. The familiar warmth of Graham's arms calms Marissa somewhat as he rubs his hands up and down her back.

Graham had always been a safe haven for Marissa growing up. Marissa's dad, Colton, passed away when she was two years old. Marissa had no memory of him, except for photos.

Like her, he was covered in freckles. Her mom often told her how much she looked like her dad, but Graham was the father Marissa knew. He was the one who was there for all her firsts, and he was always at her defense where her mom was concerned.

Sharon walks into the room, poised and as impeccably dressed as always, not a hair out of place. Her raven-black hair is pulled back perfectly from her face, exposing her high cheekbones and full lips. She's such a beauty that Graham often refers to her as his chocolate goddess. "What's all the commotion about?" she asks, hands at her side. "I heard that you called this morning, Marissa." Her tone is stern, and Marissa twists her fingers uneasily.

"Hi, Mom, umm, Mother, umm…" She half hugs her mother. Sharon's hands stay firmly at her side. "Stephen and I have some news," Marissa says nervously. Stephen holds her hand reassuringly. There is a long awkward pause as Marissa and Sharon stare at each other. Marissa tries to read her mother's gaze, but as usual, Sharon lets nothing slip.

"So do you plan on telling me now or over coffee?" she asks as she turns and heads to the kitchen.

"I'll take tea, Mother," Marissa responds.

Sharon turns to look at her daughter curiously, "You always drink coffee. What's changed?"

"I'll take some tea as well, honey," Graham chimes in quickly. Sharon glares at him then turns and walks away. The heels of her shoes bite excessively hard into the tiled floor.

"Stephen, I trust you are still drinking coffee?" This is her first acknowledgement of Stephen's presence. "Black, I assume, since everyone is changing these days."

"Black is fine, Sharon. Thank you," Stephen replies as they follow Sharon to the kitchen.

"Well, that started off well." Jade giggles at her sister. "Let's see if y'all can make it through tea before y'all kill each other."

"Jade-Ann Swanson, you're enjoying this a bit too much," Marissa says, laughing with her sister. They hurry after their mother toward the kitchen; Graham and Stephen follow close behind.

Marissa hears Graham making small talk with Stephen. She isn't too sure of what is being said, mainly because of the tight knot that now sits in her stomach. She's nauseous and almost faint. Not from her pregnancy, she's sure, but rather from the looming conversation.

Sharon sets coffee and tea on the table, along with her famous miniature cakes that Marissa loves. She calls them sweet fluffy pieces of heaven. She reaches for one and hums delightfully as the cake melts away in her mouth. "Mother, these are as amazing as always," Marissa says to her mom, scarfing another.

"I know," Sharon responds. "I am consistent in everything I do. That way there are no surprises." She looks at Marissa, unamused. "Now what is it my daughter has to tell me that is so important that you're nervous eating? That is your third cake."

Marissa puts the cake down. Stephen reaches over and holds her hand. Marissa looks across the table at her mom as she tries to read her face. She finally gives up trying then blurts out, "Stephen and I are pregnant!"

Sharon's jaw clenches for the briefest of moments, but as quickly as it happens, she composes herself. She stares blankly at her daughter. "Mother, did you hear what I just said? Stephen and I are pregnant!"

"I heard what you said, Marissa." She bitingly pronounces Marissa's name. Marissa takes a deep breath in anticipation. She knows what is coming just from the way her name was pronounced.

Sharon gets up from the table and walks over to the fridge, "The whole neighborhood heard what you said," Sharon continues.

Marissa walks over to her mom, "And that's all you have to say, Mom? No congratulations? No I am happy for you?"

Sharon glares at her daughter. "What exactly am I congratulating you for, Marissa?"

Graham gets up from his chair and is now standing in front of Sharon and Marissa. He has seen this scene played out a million times. He turns to his wife.

"Sharon," his tone warning, "don't."

Marissa stares at her mom in utter disbelief.

"What do you want me to say, Marissa?" Sharon's eyes flash with anger, "I told you I did not agree with the way you were trying to conceive, and now because you are pregnant, you expect me to toss my beliefs in the trash and be happy for you?"

"Mother! Why do you have to be a hundred years behind the times? Why can't you just be happy for us?" Marissa asked.

"Issa, you told her you hooked up with a stranger?" And as fast as the words leave Jade's mouth, she wishes she could pull them all the way back. Marissa glares angrily at Jade as the shock registers on their mother's face.

"Issa, I'm so sorry...I thought...I thought..."

Sharon cuts Jade off from finishing. "You left from injecting some unknown person's sperm inside of you to now spreading your legs to a complete stranger? You committed adultery? Who are you, Marissa Elizabeth Swanson? Who are you really? What have you done with my daughter? Because you are not the girl I raised!"

Stephen wheels in front of Sharon. "I will not stand here and have you disrespect my wife like this! This is mine and Marissa's decision. We are simply sharing our joy with you."

"Stand here and watch?" Sharon exclaimed angrily, "No, Stephen, you haven't stood in ages! All you do is sit there and watch as my daughter tosses her soul to eternal hell!

Graham interjects, "Sharon! Stop! That's enough! Stop this right now!"

Sharon glares at Graham and continues throwing her onslaught at Stephen. "You hide behind your chair and give in to my daughter's every whim even if it means damning her soul! No, Stephen, you have not stood at all!"

Marissa will never forget the shocked expression on everyone's faces and the hurt in Stephen's eyes.

"Wow, Mother! Just wow!" Tears roll down Marissa's face. "Let's go, Stephen! We should not be where we are not wanted or respected!" Marissa storms from the kitchen. Graham and Jade call out after her.

"Peanut, wait! Don't leave like this! Let's talk about this." Graham tries to stop his daughter.

"No, Dad! We are leaving. Mother has expressed just exactly how she feels," Marissa says through gritted teeth.

"Issa, I am so sorry," says Jade, tears streaming down her face, "I am so sorry, Sissy." Marissa hugs her sister; she kisses her tear-stained face.

"I'm not mad at you, Jae. It's okay." Marissa holds her sister's face reassuringly. "I promise I am not mad at you, but I have to go." She kisses her sister again, "I love you; we'll talk soon, I promise. We'll do lunch or something, but I gotta go, Jae. Okay?"

"I love you too, Sissy." Jade gives her sister a tight squeeze. "Yes, lunch. I'm happy for you. I'm gonna be the coolest aunt." Jade kisses her sister again then watches as she and Stephen exit.

Fire is burning in Jade's belly before they even close the door. Her caramel cheeks flushes with anger. "Mother! How can you be so cruel? Not everything is about you and the god you keep ramming down our throats," Jade says angrily. "Wait. No nastiness to hurl my way?" She waits for her mother to retaliate.

Sharon looks at Jade, disappointment evident in her eyes. She shakes her head and walks away.

"Oh, the nastiness is only reserved for Issa and Stevie? You're such a hypocrite, Mom! You and your so-called religion! I am so over it all! By the way, I saw your choir director at the club over the weekend. Go figure! Hypocrites!" she yells after her mother.

"Calm down, Jade, and do not speak to your mother like that," Graham pipes in. "Your mom is just upset. She and Marissa will work it out. They always do."

"Upset?" Jade rolls her eyes and her nostrils flare with seething anger. "And that gives her all the right to hurt and step all over Issa and Stevie's happiness?"

Her dad walks over to Jade, who is still visibly shaking, and hugs her. "They have been unhappy for so long, Daddy. If anyone deserves an ounce of happiness, it's those two. How can she rob them of that joy and then claim to be a Christian?" she cries.

"Your mother is a complicated woman. She has her beliefs, but she loves you and your sister more than anything in this world," Graham reassures his daughter. "She's just hurting right now, Jade. Give her some time to calm down."

Unbeknownst to Jade and Graham, Sharon watches from down the hall. She shakes her head and walks away.

Sharon believes her family has gone mad because no one sees what she sees. More than anything, Sharon prays daily for the souls of her husband and children, and they have just spit on all those prayers.

Chapter 4

Marissa pulls into their driveway, the engine of her SUV humming gently. She turns to look at Stephen, tears welled in her eyes.

Stephen reaches over and strokes her face gently. "Issa, baby, you can't control your mom or how she thinks." Marissa glances at him through curtains of tears. "We decided this. The decision was ours and solely ours." He reaches down and strokes her belly. "Besides, Sharon will come around when she sees this bouncing bundle of joy who will be her grandson."

Marissa half laughed, half cried. "Or granddaughter."

Stephen continues, "She or he will be every bit as perfect as you are, and no one will be able to resist, not even Sharon." Stephen wipes away the tears rolling down her cheeks. "Now can you smile for me?" He kisses her gently on the lips. "It will be fine, Issa. I promise."

Even though Marissa knows that nothing is guaranteed, somehow, she relaxes as the reassurance in Stephen's voice washes over her. "I love you, babe. You're the only person I would want to be on this journey with," Marissa says, hugging Stephen.

In that moment, she thinks of Jason. Her thought is quickly interrupted as her phone rings. Marissa reluctantly lets Stephen go and reaches for the phone. "It's Natalia," she says, showing Stephen the phone.

"Hmm" Stephen says in acknowledgement.

"Hey, Nat," Marissa says, answering her phone.

"Are you okay, Marissa? Jade called and then I received a text from Stephen," Natalia says on the other end of the line.

Marissa glanced over to Stephen curiously and mouthed the words, "You texted her? When?" Stephen shrugged his shoulders in response. "Does she know?" she mouthed and again, Stephen shrugged.

"I'm okay, Nat. How are you? I know we haven't caught up since I came back. I have been so swamped at the office, and this account I am working on…" Marissa rambles on.

"Are you free for lunch? I really need to talk," Natalia asks. Marissa hesitates for the briefest of moments. She is mentally and emotionally exhausted and just wants to take a bath and curl up in her bed, but this is Natalia, her best friend. Yes, she will make the exception.

"El Cilantro Tacos?" Marissa asks.

"Yes, we gotta do some tequila shots. It's that kinda day, girl," Natalia says. Marissa laughs, looking at Stephen.

"Alright, Nat. I'll meet you in an hour." Marissa ends the call, then turns to Stephen, relieved. "She doesn't know. She just said we needed to do some shots. I'm glad Jade didn't say anything because I want to tell her in person."

"Okay," Stephen says, shrugging his shoulders. "My neck is feeling pretty stiff anyway. I think I need to relax."

"Do you want me to stay with you, babe? I can call Nat and cancel. We can catch up another time."

Stephen rubs her leg. "No, honey, I'll be fine. I need to call Ethan anyway and share our good news. Plus, you need relaxing as well, and I believe some laughter with your girl will help you to do just that."

Marissa shuts the car off then exits and grabs Stephen's wheelchair from the trunk. She opens his door and leans in to kiss him. "You know I don't mind curling up right beside you, right? That's my favorite place in the entire world." She kisses him again.

"I know," Stephen responded between kisses, "but go hang out with Natalia. I'll be here when you get home to curl up with." Stephen settles in his chair and wheels down the stone pathway.

Marissa watches him as he opens the door and wheels himself in. As Marissa is about to get in the car, she hears Stephen's voice calling after her. "Not too much spicy food now, Issa!"

Marissa laughs at Stephen while raising her hand. She replies, "Scout's honor. By the way, say hi to Ethan for me."

"Will do my darling. Have fun!" Stephen replies as he pulls out his phone and dials Ethan's number.

Ethan was a trusted friend of Stephen and Marissa. He was in combat with Stephen and remained by their sides after Stephen's injuries. If anyone understands the haunting thoughts that plague Stephen daily, he does. "Hey, brother," Stephen says as Ethan answers the phone, "I got some news."

Ethan listens intently as Stephen shares the news of their pregnancy. "I am happy for you, brother." Ethan says with joy. "I am happy for both of you." How's Marissa doing?"

"She's well, just a bit upset about how Sharon took the news." Stephen proceeds to tell Ethan about the encounter with Sharon.

Ethan scratches the bald spot on top of his head with the three remaining fingers on his left hand. He too bears the scars of battle. His dark bear-like frame is etched with various battle scars that have healed in keloid form over the years, making the movement of his limbs a somewhat painful process.

Aside from the physical pain that he is in daily, the unseen scars are what hurts the most. "Sharon is entitled to her beliefs though, my brother." Ethan answers, "You can't take that from her. The same way you and Marissa are entitled to your happiness. The two things can exist together. It doesn't have to be one or the other."

As usual, Ethan is always right. He is a straight shooter, and Stephen has come to appreciate his directness over the years. "Well, when you put it that way." Stephen laughs, and Ethan joins him in laughter on the other end.

"All jokes aside," Ethan voice grows serious, "how are you truly handling this? It can't be easy for you. Not the way you love Marissa. The thought of her with…, even if it's just for a night…" His voice trails off.

Ethan is being direct as usual, yet there's a lot that's left unsaid in his statement, and Stephen feels the need to ensure that his friend knows that this was his idea. He would never want Ethan, or anyone as a matter of fact, to look at Marissa in any kind of disparaging way.

Stephen opts to lie in this instance. He half laughs before he responds, "I am handling it well. This was my idea. I am glad we are pregnant. I am truly excited to be a dad. We are just praying for a healthy pregnancy and a healthy baby. All good on my end, brother." Stephen rambles on, seemingly more to convince himself than Ethan.

"If you are good, I am good. Janine and I will come out to see you guys soon." Ethan replies. "In the meantime, give Marissa our love, and congratulations to you both. I am looking forward to teaching my nephew how to play ball because his daddy sucks at it." Ethan lets out a roaring laughter at Stephen's expense.

"Who says it's a boy, could be a girl as well, or both," Stephens replies, laughing.

"Boy or girl, you still suck at playing ball so I will have to rescue my nephew or my niece, otherwise they will be the butt of everyone's joke on the playground and we can't have that."

"We definitely can't have that." Stephen says, laughing, "We definitely can't have that. Thank God for Uncle Ethan!"

Still laughing, Stephen says his goodbye to his friend. He wheels himself into the living room, plops himself on the sofa and turns on the TV. He quickly switches the channel from the scene of a couple passionately kissing. He aimlessly flicks through the channels.

The thought of Marissa with some faceless man has haunted his dreams since the day she came back home. He quickly pushes it from his mind.

He looks to the liquor cabinet, but he honestly knows that even if he drinks all the wine in a bootlegger's cellar, nothing can erase the thoughts that plagues his mind.

He finally settles on a channel that shows a pack of lions hunting a buffalo. Stephen watches as the helpless animal is cornered and the lioness pounces for her kill. "Poor choice of show," he says to himself as he turns the TV off, and rests his head on the sofa, welcoming the wave of sleep that hovers over him, hopeful that his dreams will be of a certain freckled temptress and the days when he was completely whole.

***

El Cilantro Tacos is filled with the usual hustle and bustle of the regular Friday evening late lunch and after-work crowd. The amazing smell of mixed spices and herbs hangs heavily in the air. Marissa takes a good whiff as she enters. She loves this spot.

In her college days, this was one of the places that she usually hung out with Natalia. As a matter of fact, this is where she met Stephen while waiting on Natalia to arrive.

Marissa looks down at the watch on her wrist. "Seems I'm always waiting on Nat," she says with a smile.

"Not this time," says a voice. Marissa turns to see the warm smile of her friend Natalia as she engulfs her in a bear hug. "God, I missed you. We have so much to talk about," Natalia says, hugging her friend again.

"Wait a minute," Marissa says, "something is so different about you." Natalia laughs. Her face immediately turns red.

Marissa continues talking while walking around Natalia, inspecting her from head to toe. "New pants suit, red highlights in hair, nails manicured, and are those red bottoms?" Marissa asks, pointing to Natalia's open-toed black stilettos.

"You like?" Natalia asks, laughing while she does a twirl.

"I love!" Marissa exclaims. "Who are you and what have you done with my friend?" Marissa laughs while hugging her friend again. "It's really great to see you Nat."

Just then a male host walks over to them, "Welcome ladies, how many in your party?"

"Just us," Natalia responds, "but you are welcome to join."

The waiter grins shyly at Natalia. "Table or booth, ma'am?"

"Booth, Mario," Natalia says, reading the name on the waiter's name tag.

"Okay, follow me." he says.

"Anywhere." Natalia responds flirtatiously. Marissa stands in amazement, watching the exchange between Natalia and the waiter. What happened to her usually shy, reserved, extremely conservative friend?

"Ladies," Mario says, showing them to their booth, "your server will be right with you. If you need anything else, just let me know."

"We sure will, Mario," Natalia says, her tongue massaging the "r" in Mario's name. Blushing, the waiter hastily walks away.

"He's rather handsome, don't you think?" Natalia asks her friend, "A little short, but I could make it work." Natalia gazes after the departing host. Marissa looks at her friend in disbelief.

"Okay, what has gotten into you?" she asks, eyeing her friend curiously. "Most important, who has gotten into you?" Natalia's face turns crimson red as she lets out a girlie giggle. "Dish Natalia Morrison."

"There is nothing to dish," Natalia responds. Marissa glares knowingly at her friend. "Okay, fine. There's this new attorney at work." Natalia giggles.

"Go on," Marissa says impatiently, "new attorney, continue."

"Yes, new attorney. His name is Jackson, Jackson Sinclair." Natalia giggles again as she says his name. "He's brilliant, ruthless…" Marissa raises her eyebrows. Natalia quickly corrects herself. "Okay, fine, maybe ruthless is not the right word. He's driven, ambitious, gorgeous, sexy, a great kisser…"

"You kissed him? Natalia Abigail Morrison, what else did you do?" Natalia laughs at the shocked expression on Marissa's face.

"We kissed once." Marissa looks at her friend. She knows she is lying, "Fine. We kissed a few times, but gosh, he is such a good kisser. We may have made out a few times, but I promise, nothing else," she says, laughing.

"Now I see why all the new changes: hair, nails, and style. Jackson must be some really good kisser because he got you to color your hair, and not just color. Brunette red though, Nat?" Natalia threw her head back and laughed.

"Even how you laugh is flirtatious. Cool down over there, otherwise, I will have to get someone to bring a bucket of ice over here," Marissa says, laughing at her friend.

"Please do," Natalia responds, laughing. "Just make sure it's Mario." Again, her tongue rolled the "r" in his name. "Seriously though, Marissa, I haven't felt this way since I met…" Natalia catches herself quickly. "Well you know…"

"Actually, I don't know," Marissa says, "…since you met the mystery man in college?" Marissa air quoted 'mystery man.' "You have never even uttered his name, not even to me your best friend? Obviously, this mystery man still has some effect on you…"

Natalia cuts her off. "All I am saying is, I haven't felt this way in a long time. I think Jackson could be the real deal. And if he does other things the way he kisses me, girl, I'm telling you, I'll be running down the aisle with him."

Marissa laughs as she reaches across the table and holds her friend's hands. "Nat, I would love that. All I want is my friend to be happy, and if Jackson is the man to do that, then I say welcome Jackson."

Natalia smiled at her friend. "So tell me about your trip...who did you meet...and what did you do?" Natalia asked.

Now it is Marissa's turn to blush. She stirs uncomfortably in her seat and starts twirling her hair. "Well, the trip was great, and I met this…" Just then the waitress walked over.

"Ladies, can I take your order?" the very petite waitress asks.

"Dang it!" Natalia says, "They always come at the wrong time," she mumbles under her breath. "Do not forget what you were saying." She shoots a warning glare at Marissa across the table. Marissa laughs in response.

Natalia hurriedly gives her order. "I'll have the blackened fish taco combo and please bring two rounds of tequila shots for us." Marissa motioned no with her hands. "Three rounds?" Natalia asks.

"No, no tequila for me today." Marissa says, avoiding Natalia's eyes. "But I will have the same thing she is having, and I will take lemonade instead." The waitress notes their orders and quickly departs.

"Marissa Swanson-Paisley, you have never, ever passed up tequila shots, so now it is your time to dish." Natalia says, watching Marissa intently. "And make sure you leave nothing out. I want every tiny detail..." Just as Marissa is about to speak, the lawyer in Natalia surfaces. She wags her fingers, "Even the insignificant ones. Everything."

Marissa laughs at her friend, her freckled face turning red as she realizes that the spotlight is now on her. Natalia interjects again, "Wait, let's start with why you are not drinking tequila."

Again, Marissa attempts to speak and again Natalia interjects, "No, wait, scrap that. Start from the trip." Marissa laughs at the indecisiveness of her friend.

"If this is how you are in court, I feel sorry for your clients," Marissa jokes.

Natalia glares at her, "Are you gonna tell me or what?" Natalia asks impatiently.

"Are you gonna shut up so I can tell you or what?" Marissa asks, laughing with her friend.

"Fine. The floor is yours, just remember, every detail," Natalia says, laughing as Marissa rolls her eyes.

"Okay, so I arrived in Curacao on Thursday evening. Got to the hotel and I did not venture out of my room until Saturday morning."

"Why?" asked Natalia, "Were you sick?

"No, Nat. I just couldn't. I know Stephen was fine with this, but I wasn't sure if I was. I spent most of the time on the phone with Stephen with him urging me to go outdoors. Finally, Saturday morning I ventured out…"

"And that's when you met someone?" Natalia asks eagerly.

"Are you gonna let me tell the story or do you want to?" Marissa laughingly asks.

"Okay, sorry. Go."

The waitress walks over with their drinks. "Your food will be out soon. Is there anything else I can get you in the meantime?"

"No, thank you. We'll let you know," says Natalia, hurrying her away. "Okay, so Saturday and you are outdoors…" She urges Marissa to continue as she starts to chew on her nails.

Marissa laughs at the eagerness on her friend's face. "Nat, you're chewing on your well-manicured nails."

Natalia quickly pulls her fingers away from her mouth. "Don't change the subject, Marissa," she says, stomping her foot under the table impatiently.

"Okay," Marissa says, laughing. "I went outdoors, deciding to go into the town to get some shopping done. By the way, I bought you this lovely scarf. It has some vibrant colors…"

"Dang it, Marissa! I don't care about the scarf. What happened when you went outdoors?"

"Jeez, Nat, I'm getting there. Cool your heels," Marissa says, laughing. "Okay, so I got some shopping done. Went to a local beach. Mingled a bit with the natives then I had dinner at a restaurant in town. I had the crab with shrimp…"

"Marissa, does this face look like I give two flying figs what you ate?" Natalia laughs. "Just tell the dang story."

"Actually, that's what I'm doing," Marissa says, "if you would just stop interrupting. You said every detail, even the insignificant ones, and now you can't handle it. You were the same way with me when I met Stephen. Who am I fooling? You're always this way." Marissa laughs at the misery on her friend's face.

"Okay, I know, back to the story," Marissa jokes. "It was nightfall. By the time I got dinner, I knew the hotel wasn't far, so I decided to walk back. Ten minutes into the walk, I realized I must have left my phone back at the hotel, and I knew I needed to call Stephen since we only spoke earlier that morning. So I saw a phone booth along the road, and I stopped to make a call..."

"Hold up? Did you say a phone booth?" Natalia asks, making sure she heard right.

"Yes, ma'am, I did say a phone booth and stop interrupting." Marissa laughs. "Okay, where was I?"

Natalia was about to fill her in but stops herself.

"Okay, yes, the rain began to come down just as I got to the phone booth. I got in, called Stephen, and we talked for a bit then I decided to make a run for it because the rain was really starting to get heavier. So I told Stephen I would call him when I got back to the hotel. Just as I exited and started walking toward the hotel, a car pulled alongside me, and the passenger door swung open."

Natalia is completely engrossed in the story when the waitress returns and sets the food on the table. Marissa stops talking abruptly.

"Dang it!" Natalia exclaims out loud, and Marissa lets out a hearty laugh.

"Can I get you anything else?" the waitress asks.

"No, thank you. Trust me. You've done enough," Natalia says through gritted teeth. Marissa smiles sweetly at the waitress.

"What my friend is trying to say is that we will let you know." Marissa glares at Natalia. The waitress smiles and walks away. "I'm famished!" Marissa exclaims, "and these tacos look really yummy."

Natalia pulls the plate away from Marissa just as she is about to pick up her taco to start eating. "Who was in the car?" she asks, laughing at her friend. "You can have your tacos back when you finish the story."

Marissa laughs. "So you're holding my food hostage?"

"If you don't finish that story, we will be having some cold tacos, and none of us wants that," Natalia jokes.

Marissa laughs then continues the story. "So the car door flung open, and there is this really, I mean really handsome guy, telling me to get in before I catch a cold. Something about his smile was kind, so against my better judgement, I climbed into the car."

Natalia's eyes almost pop from her head. "Are you crazy? You got in the car? The Craigslist Killer is real, Marissa! You know this!" Natalia exclaims with a serious undertone while laughing.

"Shh." Marissa smacks her friend's hand from across the table. "Do you want everyone to know my business?" Marissa says, laughing.

"Sounds like Mr. Handsome Craigslist Killer is about to know all your business," Natalia says, grinning.

Marissa laughs at Natalia. "I'll have you know Jason is not a Craigslist Killer."

"Hmm, Jason, huh? Tell me more," Natalia says, intrigued.

"Not until you hand over my tacos," Marissa says, laughing.

Natalia reluctantly pushes the plate over to her and patiently sits and watches as Marissa scarfs two tacos in a matter of minutes, and then asks her for one of hers.

"Someone is unusually hungry." Natalia observes.

"Yes, that comes with eating for two," Marissa says, letting out a loud burp. Shock registers on Natalia's face then tears start a path down her cheeks.

"I hope those are tears of joy because I cannot deal with any more crap, not after the day I had today with my mother."

Natalia gets up from her side of the booth and sits beside her friend. "I'm gonna be an auntie?" she asks, still sniffling.

Marissa hugs her friend. "Yes, you're gonna be Auntie Nat." And just like her friend, tears start streaming down Marissa's face. They hug for a long time until Natalia finally pulls away.

"Stephen? Is he okay? How is he handling it?" Natalia asks.

"Stephen is excited. He's happy. He wanted this! You know that," Marissa says, wiping the last bit of tears from her face.

"What about the father, Jason? What do you know of him?" Natalia asks.

"Stephen is the father, Nat. Jason just aided the process," Marissa responds.

"Does he know that? What do you know about him? You know the lawyer in me has to tell you that he does have a legal claim as the biological father," Natalia concludes.

"He doesn't know. I know nothing of him other than he seemed to be some kind of musician. There was a guitar in his car and sheets of music in his hotel room. And, no, I don't know his last name and he doesn't know mine either. I wanted no attachment. That's what Stephen and I decided. The less we know and the less he knows the better." Marissa smiles at her friend.

"I hate to say it, Marissa, but there is attachment. You're pregnant." Natalia holds her friend's hand, "This baby makes you attached to him." She looks directly at Marissa. "I know this is what you and Stephen wanted, and I am happy for you both…"

Marissa cuts her off. "Then just be happy for us. I had a rough day today with my mom. I just want to enjoy this moment with my friend, not my attorney, okay, Nat?"

"Okay," Natalia says, still uncertain and slightly worried. But Marissa is right: this moment should be celebrated. "Congrats, Marissa, you are gonna be an amazing mom, and this little…what do you want?" Natalia asked, smiling.

"Girl, daughter," Marissa responded excitedly.

"This little girl, or boy, just in case... will be loved, loved, and then loved." Natalia hugs her friend another time then lets her go. Wiping the tears from her eyes, she takes a shot of tequila, then another and another.

"Slow down, Nat!" Marissa warned.

"I'm drinking for two," Natalia jokes. "Now tell me more about you and Craigslist Killer."

Marissa glares at her.

"Okay, fine. We'll call him Mr. Handsome for now...but only because he's a part of making me an aunt." Natalia and Marissa laugh.

"Well, Mr. Handsome should also be called Mr. Hot Lips, Mr. Hot Body, Mr. Good with His Hands, and Mr. Knows My Body Like A Pro."

Natalia's eyes widen.

"Yep," Marissa continues, "all those and then some." The thought of Jason has Marissa's body tingling. Her face is on fire at the thought of him exploring her.

"Marissa Swanson-Paisley, you have feelings for him!" Natalia says, daring her friend to tell her differently.

"No, I don't!" Marissa says, looking away from Natalia.

"Then what's this I am seeing written all over your face?" Natalia asks.

"Nat, you know I love Stephen. It's just that Jason made my body come alive again. I felt things I have never felt before and other things that I have not felt in years." Tears were stinging Marissa's eyes. Between the pregnancy and the look on her friend's face, she knows she is about to unravel in a ball of emotional mess.

Natalia hugs her friend to her. "You can have my other taco," she says sniffling.

Marissa laughs at her friend's quirkiness. She knows that she is truly blessed to have Natalia's friendship. "I think I might throw up if I take another bite," Marissa says still hugging Natalia. "Plus, I think you should eat something after those three shots that you just swallowed."

Natalia laughs, "You're probably right. I am already feeling hot and bothered. Not sure if it's the liquor or the story of Mr. Hot Lips, Hot Body, Mr. Hot Everything." Natalia and Marissa laugh as Marissa pushes the taco over to her.

"He had my toes curling almost four times that night," Marissa shares as Natalie almost chokes on her taco.

Between coughs she mutters, "Details, Issa, details."

Marissa laughs at the eager look on her friend's face. "Let's just say he masterfully took me to places that I did not know exist." Marissa feels that familiar longing in her body as she remembers her body entwined with Jason's as they raced towards the blissfully unknown.

"Earth to Issa. Earth to Issa!" Natalia says, jolting her friend back to the present. "You're hopelessly in love with this man, Marissa." Natalie says laughing but feeling worried at the same time.

"I most definitely am not!" Marissa says a bit too quickly. "I have not had… you know… in years." She reassures her friend, "It felt great to be desired and feel desire…" Her eyes plead at her friend for some understanding.

Natalia touches her hands reassuringly, "I understand, Issa. You deserve to feel all the feels and then some," she says, laughing at her friend, "I am grateful for Mr. Hot Whatever because Jade and I were gonna buy a broom to dust the cobwebs from your…"

"Natalia Abigail Morrison!" Marissa exclaims, cutting off Natalia before she could finish her sentence. "You and my sister are insufferable," she says, laughing as her friend hugs her tightly.

"I'm truly happy for you, Issa." Natalia hugs her friend even more tightly.

"It means the world to me, Sissy." Marissa says. "Now, if you can loosen your grip just a tad bit. You're crushing your niece or nephew. Natalia kisses Marissa's cheek as they both laugh.

Chapter 5

The morning sickness is about gone now that Marissa is well into her fourth month of pregnancy. She is slowly getting used to the idea of becoming a mother. Stephen is already awake. Marissa can hear him moving around downstairs.

Stephen has been in full prep mode since they learned of Marissa's pregnancy. He and his dad have already started clearing out the room next to theirs and have been moving everything downstairs to the spare room.

When Marissa and Stephen bought their four-bedroom home, the intent was to fill it with children. She smiles at the memory of Stephen carrying her up the stairs to their bedroom to get started on making their "squad" as he would often joke.

Marissa wanted to sell the house after Stephen's accident and get one smaller and without stairs, but Stephen was insistent on keeping the house.

His dream was to have his kids sliding down the stairs, and even after he realized he could no longer father children of his own, Stephen would not rob Marissa of the joy of the reality of that dream.

Marissa drags herself to a seated position in the bed. These days sleep is a precious commodity and making it all the way to the bathroom before her bladder gives out is even more precious. Today is not one of those days.

She can already feel the wetness in her underwear. She races from the bed and plops down on the toilet. Eyes closed, sighs of release escapes her, as she empties her bladder. Relief washes over her.

Marissa opens her eyes and looks down. "Is that blood?" she asks herself out loud. Marissa checks the toilet. Everything is red, "No! No! No! No! This is not happening! Stephen!" Marissa bellows Stephen's name at the top of her lungs.

Stephen drops the box of books that was on his lap as soon as he hears Marissa yell his name. The panic in her voice is giving him chills. He wheels himself toward the stairlift as fast as he is able, and in one fluid movement, he is on. He presses the button for the lift to move before he even straps himself in. The stairlift is agonizingly slow.

If Marissa were dying at this very moment, he could do nothing to save her. Stephen knew he could have dragged himself up the stairs much faster than the lift.

In moments like these, Stephen wishes he could rewind the clock and choose differently that day. Who is he kidding anyway? The girl with the raven black hair and the young private still haunt his dreams. Yes, he would have still made the same choice.

Finally, Stephen reaches the top of the stairs and wheels toward Marissa. He finds her in the bathroom on the floor, curled up in a ball, crying. "Issa, what's wrong, honey?" Before she could respond, Stephen sees the blood in the toilet. He wheels to the bedroom, grabs the phone, and calls 911.

Marissa's mind is numb as she listens to Stephen giving instructions to the 911 operator. *This can't be happening. I'm in some weird dream and I am going to wake up any minute now.*

Stephen reaches down and pulls her from the floor, "Honey, they are coming. Can you stand?"

"Yep, not a dream," Marissa says out loud.

Stephen looks at her, pain filling his eyes. He can't panic at this moment as it would do none of them any good. He holds her face. "Issa, it will be okay. They are coming, and the baby is fine."

"You don't know that, Stephen!" Marissa lashes out. "You don't know that! I am bleeding! That only means one thing!" She starts crying even harder. Stephen rubs Marissa's back as he pulls her onto his lap.

"Okay, baby, I'll have faith for both of us. It will be okay. Just breathe, okay?" He wipes Marissa's face. "Are you in pain? Are you contracting?"

"No," she says between tears. "I thought it was pee on my underwear. Stephen, what if I've lost our baby? Then all of this would have been for nothing! OMG! I am being punished! My mom was right! I went outside of my marriage! I am being punished and now that mistake is going to cost us our baby! This is like David and Bathsheba all over again!"

"Who?" Stephen asks, clueless as to who David and Bathsheba were.

"David and Bathsheba from the Bible. God took their baby because David committed adultery," Marissa cried.

"Listen, Issa, calm down. You're not being punished. I have no idea who David and Bathsheba are but what I know is that we are not them. You did nothing wrong. If anything, we…" he points to himself and her, "we did this. We made this decision together so any punishment would be on both of us. Stop worrying about your mom, just calm down so we can keep the baby calm. We did nothing wrong. You're letting Sharon get in your head. Just breathe. Okay, honey?"

Stephen hears the doorbell. "That must be the paramedics. Let's go. I'll call Dr. Bland and our parents from the ambulance."

Marissa slides off Stephen's legs. "Call Nat. I need Nat." She grabs the robe hanging on the bathroom door, and they make their way down the stairs.

Inside the ambulance, Marissa listens as Stephen calls Dr. Bland then their parents and then Natalia. "She'll be fine, Natalia," Stephen says, "just meet us there." His voice went lower, but Marissa could still hear him, "Listen, no tears, okay, Natalia? I cannot handle both of you crying at the same time. Okay? I'll see you there."

"Is she okay?" Marissa asks Stephen.

"She will be." Stephen says reassuringly, "You know your friend. It doesn't take much to make her cry." Stephen grins at Marissa.

Soon Marissa and Stephen are at the hospital. In the frenzy of blood being drawn, blood pressure being taken, ultrasound, and connecting her to heart monitors for her and the baby, Marissa looks across at Stephen. She can tell he is nervous, but he is doing a good job of hiding it.

Just then, Marissa hears her name being called. It's Jade. Her sister enters in tattered jeans, a tribal print T-shirt, and a headscarf. Marissa recognizes the headscarf; it is one she brought back from Curacao for her sister. If it's anything African, Jade loves it.

"Issa, are you okay? Is the baby okay?" Concern floods Jade's face as she looks at the wires attached to Marissa. Jade wraps her arms around her sister.

"We don't know yet. We are waiting on Dr. Bland," Stephen responds. Jade turns and gives Stephen a big hug.

"How are you, big bro?" she asks.

Stephen shrugs his shoulders. "I just need Marissa and the baby to be well, that's all." He fights back the tears, and Jade hugs him.

"It will be alright. Have faith. I prayed all the way over here," Jade says.

"You? Praying?" Marissa asks her sister, smiling.

"Yes, this heathen..." Jade air-quoted the word heathen,' "does know how to pray." She laughs. "Contrary to Mom's popular belief. By the way, Dad is on his way here," Jade says matter-of-factly.

"Mom?" asks Marissa.

Jade turns away and starts fidgeting with the pen on the cart next to Marissa's bed. "I believe she's at one of her women's group thingies, but I am sure she'll be here."

Marissa doesn't have time to process what she feels where her mother is concerned because Dr. Bland walks in.

"Marissa, Stephen, my two favorite people, how are you?"

Before Stephen or Marissa can answer, Jade asks, "Dr. Bland, is everyone your favorite person? Because you say that to me every time I go to your office." Jade laughs at Dr. Bland.

"Jade-Ann," Dr. Bland says laughing, her accent thick, "my favorite person. And how are you?" Dr. Bland and Sharon are the only two people who call Jade by Jade-Ann and Jade hates it.

Stephen butts in, "Dr. Bland, any update? Is the baby okay?" Marissa and Stephen stare hopefully at Dr Bland.

Dr. Bland smiles. "Yes, she is fine."

Stephen, still uncertain, asks, "Yes, Marissa is fine, or yes, the baby is fine?" Stephen asks.

"Wait! Does that mean, I am having a niece?" Jade asks.

They all turn to look at Dr. Bland. "Yes, Marissa and the baby are fine." To Jade she says, "And yes, you are having a niece."

Marissa and Stephen hug while Jade does a little dance in the corner.

Just then Graham and Natalia walked in, and Jade announces, "It's a girl! I am having a niece!"

"Are you okay, Peanut?" asks Graham. "You scared me something fierce."

"I'm alright, Daddy, and your granddaughter is too."

Graham kisses Marissa on the forehead. "I'm glad you both are okay." He says, "I'll go call your mom."

Natalia walks over as Graham exits. "So a niece, huh?" she says, hugging her friend.

"Yes, Auntie Nat, you're getting a niece," Marissa says through tears.

Dr. Bland, interjects. "Okay, we are going to keep you overnight for observation, but we have to take it easy over the next couple months. We don't want another scare like this. More rest and try to keep all stressful situations at bay."

"Aka, Mother," Jade says under her breath, but not before Marissa and Stephen catch it. They both laugh.

"Stephen, make sure she rests," Dr. Bland says as she is departing, "Jade-Ann, give my love to your mom. Tell her I'll see her at the Simpson's Charity Ball."

Jade makes a face as Dr. Bland exits.

"So how do you feel Issa?" Jade asks, "Aww... you're having a daughter, Sissy." Tears fill Jade's eyes.

"No, Jae," Marissa laughs, "I'm not doing the tears with you, especially since the queen of crying is present." Marissa motions to a laughing Natalia.

"I'll go get you some water," Stephen says, excusing himself from the room.

"So what happened, Marissa?" Natalia asks.

"I went to pee, and there was blood on my panties, and I looked in the toilet, and it was filled with blood, and I completely lost it. I'm just glad the baby is okay."

"You know that just a little bit of blood will color the water in the toilet, so it seems like a lot of blood, right?" Jade asks, laughing at her sister. "I think you panicked."

"Jade-Ann Swanson, I'm not playing with you." Marissa laughed. "If you knew how scared I was you wouldn't make a joke of this," Marissa says, playfully slapping her sister. "Plus, Stephen, OMG, he was white as a sheet. Like dad kinda white." Marissa, Jade, and Natalia laugh.

"Dad needs to get some color on them legs," Jade jokes.

Graham reenters the room. "What's wrong with my legs, ladies?" Graham laughs. "I'll have you know my wife likes them just as they are."

"Ewww, Dad! Don't be gross," Jade says, laughing.

Graham kisses Marissa's head. "I spoke to your mom. She's at a meeting. She's glad you are okay though."

"Thanks, Daddy," Marissa says, a hint of sadness in her voice. Marissa's secret hopes that her mom will rush to the hospital to be with her at such a time are dashed, but she isn't surprised.

"Anytime, Peanut," Graham responds. "So Stephen said you will be here overnight. I am gonna run out and get you some food. Just tell me what you want."

"Daddy, you don't have to do that. We'll be fine." Marissa smiles at her dad.

"Will you allow me to just be dad and do something for my daughter and granddaughter? What happened made me a nervous wreck. Doing something will help to calm my nerves. I'll call Nathan on my way out. I know him and Cathryn are heading over."

"You're always a nervous wreck, Daddy." Jade and Marissa laugh. Graham laughs, shaking his head at them.

As Graham walks towards the hospital exit, he sees Sharon coming out of the chapel. "You're here! But we just spoke on the phone, and you were at your women's meeting?"

Sharon smiles at Graham, "I have been here since Jade called. I just stayed in the chapel instead."

Graham hugs his wife, "Why don't you go in so that your daughter can know that you're here? I'm sure she would love that."

"Are they okay…? She looks at Graham, concern on her face.

"Yes, your daughter and granddaughter are doing fine."

"It's a girl?" Sharon asked with excitement, but as soon as she says it, the unexpected emotions quickly disappear.

"Yes," Graham says, kissing her on the cheeks. "I'm heading to get them some food. I'll see you at home?"

Sharon nods and watches as Graham walks away.

"And Sharon...," Graham says turning back towards his wife, "it's okay to be happy. This is a happy moment. You're about to be a grandmother. Celebrate that." Sharon looks at him with some sadness then turns and walks back into the chapel.

Stephen is at the vending machine getting a drink. Natalia walks over to him. "Umm...how have you been, Stephen?

Stephen turns to see Natalia; she gives him a long lingering hug. He finally pulls away. "I've been fine. How are you?"

"Stephen, it's me...really, how are you?" Natalia asked insistently.

"What can I say? I am excited we are finally having a baby. You know how that has been."

"Yeah, I know, but how are you handling it? This cannot be easy." Stephen looks at her. "And don't tell me about Marissa, I want to hear about you."

"I'm fine, Natalia. Marissa is happy and that's all that matters," He says sharply.

"You can't keep this bottled in. You used to tell me everything."

"What exactly do you want me to say to you, Natalia? That I am sorry that I forced my wife to sleep with another man so she could make a baby I couldn't give her? Is that what you're waiting to hear?" Stephen glares angrily at Natalia. His voice grows louder. "Well you won't hear that from me. I love Marissa and her happiness is all that matters, and this baby will bring her the happiness I can no longer give her. How I feel about it is a nonissue! And, yes, I can keep it bottled up inside! You taught me that!"

Through clenched teeth Natalia responds, "This is not about us. This is about you and Marissa!"

"You continue telling yourself that, Natalia, if it makes you feel better. When we slept together that night, I did not know Marissa then. I met her after, and yes, I fell in love with her. When I realized you two were best friends, I wanted to tell her about us, but you decided that we should not as it would ruin your friendship. You decided that, not me! At least this is something that I have decided, so please spare me the bull about keeping things bottled up. You're the queen of that."

Stephen wheels away. She watches silently as he rolls down the hall. In all the years she's known Stephen, she has never seen him this angry, and they have never spoken about the night they made love. Natalia has tried putting that night behind her, but unfortunately, Stephen is the one that holds her heart just as Marissa is the one that holds his. Natalia composes herself and follows Stephen back to Marissa's room.

Just outside the chapel door unbeknownst to Natalia and Stephen, Sharon watches the exchange.

Natalia enters the room to see that Cathryn and Nathan have joined the other visitors. Jade and Cathryn are deep in conversation, and Stephen and Nathan are laughing about something. Marissa looks up to see Natalia. "Where's the coffee? I thought you were getting coffee for you and Jade."

Natalia fumbles for an answer… "Err...the machine wasn't working...the coffee here probably isn't any good anyway." Natalia walks over and hugs Cathryn and Nathan.

"We have to get you out of here real soon, Rissy," Jade says. "Coffee machine is not working, and neither is the soda machine. This place is practically falling apart."

Natalia and Stephen carefully avoid each other's eyes.

"Marissa, I have to go. I'm still prepping for that big case I told you about," Natalia says, kissing her friend goodbye. She hugs everyone else in the room, except for Stephen, and exits. Marissa doesn't miss that. She looks across to Stephen; he's scowling.

What's going on with those two? Marissa wonders.

"Marissa, I'll make sure to drop off meals for you. I need you to relax so that my granddaughter can stay in that little oven and bake properly," Cathryn says, rubbing Marissa's belly.

"You don't have to do that, Cathy. Stephen and I can manage but thank you." Marissa says.

"It's useless, Marissa. Cathryn has been itching to fuss over you from the day she found out you were pregnant. Unfortunately, she won't give up," Nathan says, kissing his daughter-in-law. "Especially now that she knows it is a granddaughter like she wanted, you won't be able to be rid of her."

Stephen laughs in agreement. "Thanks, Mom. I'll ensure she rests up."

"Then it's settled," Cathryn says, kissing her son. "Come on, Nathan, we have some shopping to do."

Nathan hugs his son. "You don't know what you have just unleashed on me. She will never stop." Nathan makes a face as Cathryn slaps him playfully.

"Bye, Issa. Bye, Zuri," Jade says, rubbing her sister's belly.

"Wait... who is Zuri?" Marissa asks, laughing.

"My niece of course," Jade says. "It is Swahili for beauty, and with you as her mother, she will be beautiful."

"I think you just threw that part in there to make the case for your choice of name," Marissa says, laughing. "but Stephen and I will decide, and we will let you know your niece's name soon."

"Fine. You can't blame me for trying." Jade laughs. "Bye, big bro. Take care of these two for me." She kisses Stephen as she exits.

Alone at last, Stephen rubs Marissa's belly as he sings to it. "Te amo mi amor te amo eres hermosa mi amor, tan hermosa."

"She's gonna come out singing in Spanish," Marissa says to Stephen.

"At least you'll have a live-in translator." Stephen kisses her. "You scared me today, honey. I'm glad you and the baby are okay."

"I scared me today too." Marissa says, kissing Stephen, "but I am thankful that you were there, still here, helping me through it."

Stephen kisses her, "Where else would I be, ssa? You're my whole heart. There is nowhere else I would be." Stephen hugs Marissa and resumes singing, his time in English, "I love you my love, I love you, you are beautiful my love, so beautiful." The soothing sound of Stephen's calming voice lulls Marissa, and she slowly drifts off to sleep.

CHAPTER 6

Marissa is excited; she is just weeks away from her due date. Stephen and Nathan have worked hard putting the finishing touches on the baby's room.

She has some last-minute shopping to do and plans on meeting up with Jade and Natalia to get that done. She kisses Stephen goodbye and heads downstairs to get her keys to leave. She walks in the kitchen and reaches for the keys.

"So how are you handling this now that the baby will be here soon?" Nathan asks. Marissa turns to see the baby monitor on the kitchen table. Her first instinct is to turn off the monitor; she does not want to intrude on Nathan and Stephen's private conversation. "What will you do if the baby looks like whoever the father is and not Marissa?"

"I won't say it will be easy, Dad, but I love Issa. Any child of hers is mine, so I have learned to deal with it," Stephen responds.

"Stephen, I will never understand you. You are a way bigger man than me. The thought of Cathryn being with another man infuriates me to my very core. I don't understand how you tolerated it."

"Issa wasn't with another man like that, Dad. It wasn't something she enjoyed doing. I know you don't understand this, and I am not asking you to understand, but Issa shouldn't have to settle for someone injecting her with someone's frozen sperm to make a baby, because me, her husband, is not man enough to do so."

"Stephen, Marissa doesn't look at you like that; she loves you. You are the one who is looking at yourself as less than a man."

"I know, Dad. Like I said, you won't understand, so let's just drop it."

"Stephen, you can't keep these things bottled up."

"Dad, I really don't wanna have this conversation. You sound like Natalia. Can we just finish putting the crib together?"

"What if this guy surfaces, Stephen? Then what?"

"Dad," Stephen's tone warns, "drop it, please?"

Marissa turns off the monitor, deciding that she has heard more than she needed to. Now she wonders what Stephen meant that Nathan sounded like Natalia. She tries not to dwell on it.

She gets in her car and starts to drive, yet Stephen and Nathan's conversation has left her stomach feeling uneasy. She thinks of Jason. *Where is he? Does he think of me at all?*

Marissa wishes she had gotten Jason's last name. At least she would have been able to stalk him on Facebook or Instagram if he had an account. She rubs her belly, wondering if the baby will look like Jason.

Her mind races to Stephen. This should have been their child. *Life can be so cruel at times.* One thing she is sure about is that Stephen loves her and will love their baby even though he is not her biological father.

***

The mall is bustling with shoppers as Marissa arrives at the food court where she promised to meet Jade and Natalia. She spots her always Afrocentric sister and walks over to her. "What are you devouring this time?" She kisses the top of her sister's head.

"Nothing that you'd eat," Jade says, laughing.

"You're right. It looks gross." Marissa takes a seat across from her sister. She reaches across to sample the food on Jade's plate. "It tastes gross too."

"What's gross?" Natalia asks. She hugs Jade, then Marissa. "Eww," she says as she sees Jade's plate. "What is that?"

"First of all, it is seaweed, mushroom, and quinoa stir fry…," Jade laughs as they both make a face, "and second of all, it's delicious. Marissa, you should be eating clean for my niece."

"Unfortunately, your niece needs meat, lots and lots of red meat. What's that you're saying, baby girl?" She rubs her tummy as if hearing from the baby, "You want a burger? Okay, Mom will get you that." Marissa laughs.

"Medium-well, with large fries and chocolate milkshake?" Natalia asks.

"See?" Marissa laughs at Jade. "Even Auntie Nat is hearing from the baby. Make that a chocolate vanilla shake, Nat. I feel like walking on the wild side today."

"We're gonna have to roll you out of here when you're done." Jade laughs as Natalia departs to get the food.

"So how is our mother?" Marissa asks. "Are you two at least talking to each other?

"We are civil, but we haven't spoken much since you and Stephen were last there."

"Both of us can't be mad at her, Jae. I know she acts tough, but she needs one of us. At least you. Every time Mom and I have an argument, I don't worry much because I know she has you." Marissa reaches for her sister's hand.

"That's a lot of responsibility to put on me though, Issa, and right now it is hard to forgive her. I'm still shocked at how she treated you and Stephen."

"Well, technically, it got worse after you told her I had a one-night stand." Marissa laughs at her sister.

"Don't remind me, Issa. I feel horrible about that day."

"I told you that I wasn't mad at you. Listen, I would have ten one-night stands if it means experiencing the joy of this little one growing inside me." Marissa rubs her belly gently. "I'm so in love with her already, and I haven't even met her yet."

Jade gets up and sits beside her sister. She gently rubs her belly. "Auntie loves Princess Zuri." She speaks to Marissa's belly.

"Umm... about that name…" Marissa stops short as the TV screen overhead catches her attention; she gasps in shock as she sees the face on the screen.

"Are you okay, Issa? Is it the baby?" Jade asks, sensing the change in Marissa.

"Ummm...ummm...Jason…?"

"What...who is Jason? Issa, you're not making any sense."

"What's the matter?" Natalia asks, "Is it the baby?

"I don't know. She's just...I don't know?" Jade stutters, trying to make sense of Marissa's reaction.

Marissa sits staring at the screen, her mouth wide open, a shocked expression on her face.

Jade and Natalia turn to see what is affecting Marissa so much. On the screen overhead, a man is being interviewed for an upcoming concert in Nashville. The caption on the screen reads: *Country Superstar Jason Saunders to perform at Nashville Under the Stars Valentine concert.*

"Wow! Jason Saunders," Marissa mutters; she finally knows what his last name is.

"Who is Jason Saunders, and why do you look like you've seen a ghost, Issa?" Jade asks.

"Wait!" Natalia says, her brain finally catching up with what was going on. "Is Jason Saunders the Jason? As in Mr. Hot Lips? Mr. Handsome And Then Some Jason?" She is just as shocked as Marissa.

"Y'all better explain what is going on because both of you are…Wait!" The lightbulb finally clicks in Jade's head. "Jason Saunders is your one-night stand?" Jade looks at her sister with a mixture of humor, fascination, and admiration. "OMG, you hooked up with Jason Saunders! As in country superstar Jason Saunders! As in that hottie on the screen?"

"Why don't you say it louder so the people across the mall at the Victoria's Secret shop can hear you?" Marissa grits her teeth.

Jade lowers her voice to a loud whisper, "Of all the people in the world, and you hook up with Jason Saunders!" Jade could not stop laughing. "I bet you had no clue who he was." Jade laughs even harder. "Issa, you gotta tell me, how was he? I mean, he's hot. Come on, you gotta share...wait...my niece's father is the Jason Saunders?"

Marissa is red in the face. "Stephen Paisley is your niece's father, not Jason! Don't you ever say that again Jae, I'm serious!" Marissa turns Jade's face to her. "Jae, I am serious. It would crush Stephen if he ever heard you say that, plus he doesn't know who I hooked up with and I would rather keep it at that. Are you listening, Jae? You and Nat are the only two people who know, and it stays between us. Do you understand that?"

She looks at Jade and at Natalia. She repeats herself, "This stays between- Whoa! OMG! Whoa!" Marissa grimaces.

"What's wrong, Issa?" Jade and Natalia ask, concern in their voices.

Natalia looks down as water splashes at her feet. She freezes as she looks at Marissa.

"Whoa!" Jade exclaims. "Is that what I think it is?"

"I think my water broke," Marissa says in a calm, yet panicked voice.

"What do we do? What do we do? Issa, what do we do?" Jade asks, frantically moving around.

Marissa grips her sister's hand. "First, you're gonna stay calm."

"Calm. Okay, I got that...calm. I am calm, very calm. I'm zen even. I'm finding my center," Jade says, closing her eyes.

"Okay, Jae, focus!" Marissa says through gritted teeth. "Unzen… then you're gonna call Stephen and tell him to meet us at the hospital. Natalia, you call Dr. Bland and let her know what's happening. On second thought, Jade, you call Mom and Dad, and Natalia, you call Stephen and then Dr Bland."

Natalia and Jade nod. "So who is gonna call the ambulance?" Jade asks.

"We are close to the hospital so Natalia can drive us. My car is parked in a spot reserved for mothers. Okay, everybody…. Whoa! Ouch! Everybody got it? Aaaaghhh! Marissa clutches the edge of the table as a wave of contractions rock her body.

"We got it! We got it!" Jade says, "I need a phone! Gotta find a phone."

"How about using the phone in your hand?" Marissa says through clenched teeth. "This is why Nat is the one calling Stephen and Dr. Bland because I know you would lose it," Marissa says, laughing through her pain.

"I'm not losing it," Jade says nervously. "It's not every day your big sister goes into labor."

"I would hope not, because this pain is so- Aaaaghhh!" She grips the table tighter. "Nat, I need Stephen...I need Stephen. I can't do this without him."

"I'll call him on our way out," Natalia says, holding on to her friend as she leads her towards the exit.

Marissa looks back at the TV screen overhead. Jason's face fills the screen. Marissa realizes that she is about to give birth to the baby they both so passionately made. "I need Stephen, Nat. I really do."

"I'm calling him now, Issa." Natalia holds on to her friend as another wave of contractions washes over her.

Stephen and Nathan are admiring their handiwork. The crib and changing table are now fully assembled. "This is perfect. All that is missing is my granddaughter," Nathan says in satisfaction.

"Dad, can you treat the baby as if she shares your DNA? Will you be able to do that?" Stephen asks his father. "Even if she does not look like Marissa?"

A hurt expression crosses Nathan's face. "Stephen, this baby is my granddaughter. It's your child. I did not ask you that question earlier because I am having an issue loving my granddaughter. Quite the opposite in fact. I am already in love with and can't wait to meet her."

Just then Stephen's phone rings. Stephen looks and sees it is Natalia and sends it to voicemail.

Immediately, the phone rings again. Stephen hesitates but decides to answer just in case something is wrong with Marissa.

"Stephen," Natalia says as soon as Stephen answered, "Can you meet us at the hospital, or should I send Jade for you? Marissa is in labor!"

"What! What happened? No, I'm fine. Dad is here. He'll take me! Is Issa okay? Is the baby okay?"

"Yes, she's fine, they are both fine. Jade and I are taking her. Her water broke but she's okay. I'll let you know as soon as we get there."

"Okay, let me talk to her." Stephen hears Marissa's voice on the phone. "Honey, are you okay?"

"I'm fine, babe. Just aaagghh! Just get here, Stephen!"

"Okay, honey, just breathe. Dad and I are on our way."

"I am breathing!" Marissa says through clenched teeth.

"Okay, Issa. I love you. You're my whole heart, and I'll see you soon. Bye." Stephen hangs up the phone and turns to his dad, a big grin on his face, "Well, Grandpa, you're about to meet your granddaughter! Issa's water broke, and they are heading to the hospital. We have to meet them there."

"Okay, son, let's go!"

Stephen is already wheeling for the stairs.

"Wait! Where is the overnight bag! I've heard Marissa speak so much of that bag," Nathan says.

"Aah, yes. You are right!" He quickly disappears into their bedroom and emerges with the bag on his lap. Once again, the stair climber takes forever to get to the bottom. Nathan locks up behind Stephen and wheels him to the car.

"We can call your mom from the car. She would kill us if she missed this."

Stephen chuckles, "Yes, we'd both be dead." Nathan and Stephen laugh.

***

Marissa screams as sweat drips from her forehead. Stephen wipes the moisture away. Her legs are propped up as Dr. Bland instructs her what to do. Marissa tries to focus on something in the room to take away the pain that threatens to rip her whole body apart. *The light. Focus on the light.*

"You're doing good, honey," Stephen says, encouraging Marissa.

"I can't, honey. I can't. I'm too tired. It hurts, Stephen. It hurts really, really, really bad."

I know Issa, but you got this. You're the strongest, bravest, most beautiful woman that I know. You totally got this." Stephen kisses her sweat-slicked forehead.

"Okay, Marissa," says Dr. Bland, "I know this is hard, but you are just a few minutes away from holding your precious little girl in your arms. Come on, a few more big pushes, and that will get us there."

"You got this," Jade says, grimacing in the corner. "Why did I decide that I wanted to be in the room? I feel like I am about to faint."

"Sit down, Jade-Ann," Dr Bland says, "We can't have you fainting in here. Or maybe you should go get some fresh air."

Jade looks at Marissa and Stephen as if asking for permission. They both motion to her to go.

"Chicken," Marissa says, chuckling through her pain. She squeezes Stephen's hand as the pain radiates through her body.

"I'm no chicken, but ewww, what is that?" Jade asks.

"Go, Jade-Ann," says Dr. Bland. "We have a baby to deliver."

Jade exits to the sounds of Marissa's screams. She barely makes it to the waiting room and collapses on a chair.

"Is she okay?" Natalia asks.

"What about the baby?" Cathryn and Nathan chime in.

"Are you okay, princess?" Graham asks.

Jade puts up her hand as if to quiet everyone. "Wait...shhh...I just need to catch my breath and settle my stomach," Jade says, trying not to gag.

"I'll go see what's happening," Natalia says.

"Well, let's hope your stomach is stronger than mine," Jade says.

Natalia walks off as Jade turns to Cathryn, Nathan, and Graham to let them know that Marissa is doing fine and that the baby isn't here yet.

Natalia knocks and enters the delivery room, "Is it okay if I come in? Jade came out, so I figured you may need a replacement."

Marissa reaches for her friend's hand. Natalia stands on the opposite side of the bed and reaches out to Marissa. She barely looks at Stephen, and he does not acknowledge her.

Marissa catches the indifference between them. "Listen, I don't know what is going on with you two, but you both better fix it before this baby is born. I will not have my best friend and husband at odds with each other, especially with a new life coming into this world. I will need both of you." She looks at Stephen and Natalia. Barely catching her breath, she asks, "Are we clear?" They both nod in agreement.

"Okay, Marissa, give me a big push," Dr. Bland says.

Mustering all the strength she had left, Marissa screams at the top of her lungs as she pushes down. The sound of a baby's cry pierces the air and fills every inch of the delivery room. It's the most beautiful sound Marissa has ever heard.

Tears of joy flood down her face at the sound of her daughter's cry.

"Congratulations, Mr. And Mrs. Paisley, you have a beautiful daughter. Come on, Stephen, do the honors." Stephen takes the scissors from Dr. Bland and cuts the umbilical cord.

He looks at the little wet perfection, kicking and screaming in Dr. Bland's hand, and he instantly falls in love.

Dr. Bland hands the baby to Marissa. Marissa kisses the softness of the top of her head; she looks at her. She is perfectly freckled and has the most beautiful eyes.

Marissa looks up at Stephen, tears streaming down his face. "That's your daddy," Marissa says, handing the baby to Stephen. "And the person with the big smile on her face is your Auntie Nat." Stephen kisses the baby's fingers and feet, and then kisses Marissa.

"She's perfect, honey, just like her mommy." Stephen grins at Marissa. Natalia walks over, and Stephen hands her the baby.

"OMG! My niece is the most beautiful baby in the world. Oh, Issa, thank you! I'm so happy I got to share in this experience," Natalia says, smiling at her friend.

"Actually, thank Jade. She couldn't handle the blood and gore of childbirth." Natalia laughs with her friend.

"Okay, that's enough gushing for the time being." Dr. Bland says, interrupting the doting of the baby. "We have to get her cleaned up. We'll get her vitals done and return her back to you shortly."

"Wait, you're taking her?" Marissa and Stephen exclaim at the same time.

"Just to get cleaned up and checked. She'll be back by the time you're settled in your room." Dr. Bland hands the baby to the nurse in the room.

"I'll let Jade and your parents know." Natalia excuses herself from the room as Dr Bland starts to attend to Marissa.

"So have you decided on a name yet?" Dr. Bland asks.

Stephen and Marissa smile at each other, "We've selected the name Jasmine," Marissa says, holding Stephen's hand. "Doesn't she look like a Jasmine?" Marissa asks Stephen.

"She is as beautiful and delicate as jasmine. Yes, she is a Jasmine," Stephen agreed.

"Jasmine Zuri Paisley. That's her name." Marissa looks over at the baby. The nurse tags Jasmine's foot then carries her over for Marissa and Stephen to kiss goodbye before placing her back in the cart and heading to the nursery.

"See you soon, my sweet Princess Jasmine." Stephen says as they watch the nurse disappear from the room.

"Are you okay, honey?" Stephen asks Marissa, "I'm so proud of you. You did great. You're truly phenomenal, and I am grateful I experienced the newness of life with you."

Marissa kisses Stephen, "I'm fine, tired. A whole human baby just came out of me, far bigger than a poppy seed" she says, laughing, "but I am fine, mainly because you were here with me."

"No place I'd rather be, Issa." Stephen kisses her hand. "I didn't know there was space to fit anyone else in my heart because my whole heart has belonged to you since the day I met you, and now Jasmine enters and she has my heart too, so now you both share my whole heart." Stephen kisses Marissa as tears stream down her face. "I love you." He whispers, "Thank you for my daughter."

"I love you too, baby," Marissa says sleepily. Stephen watches as she drifts off to sleep.

CHAPTER 7

Graham walks in the house. Sharon is sitting in the living room, and he approaches her. "Our daughter gave birth today to her first and what may be her only child, and her mother wasn't present." Graham looks at Sharon, hurt evident in his eyes. "I'm disappointed in you, Sharon." Sharon sits there motionless. "Everyone was there except you, Sharon. Stephen's parents were there, Jade was there, Natalia was there, and the one person who I think Marissa really wanted to be there was not there. When are you going to end this standoff with your daughter? When are you going to recognize that she needs you and start being the mother that you are supposed to be to your daughter?"

Sharon glares at Graham, "Don't you dare question what kind of mother I am to my daughter!" Sharon stands and walks over to Graham. "I'm her parent and it has been that way since Colton left us. And if you must know, I already spoke to Cathryn! She told me that Marissa and the baby are doing okay. Furthermore, I'm the last person Marissa wants to see. I would rather be here praying that all goes well with her than being there to upset her further."

"FYI Colton did not leave you! The man died for crying out loud! I'm sick of hearing you talk about Colton leaving you and Marissa. I have been her father! I took her to her first father-daughter dance! I wiped her tears when that idiot boy she dated in high school broke her heart! And I was the father who walked her down the aisle to give her to the man she loves! I have been her parent too, Sharon. When will you see that?"

Sharon repeatedly jabs a finger on Graham's chest as she answers him. "Since you know my daughter so well, Graham, you should also know that if she wanted me there, she would have asked."

Graham holds his head. "Sharon, are you listening to yourself? Are you really hearing yourself? Were you waiting for a royal invitation? Your daughter wanted you to be there, and you should have been there! It doesn't matter what differences you and Marissa may have. This is an important milestone in her life, and her mother should have been there!" Sharon rolls her eyes at Graham.

"You can roll your eyes all you want, Sharon; the truth is the truth! Why would she ask you to be there, Sharon, when the last time you saw her, you basically called her a whore? You keep hiding behind prayer, but God is a God of love and forgiveness. If you're serving God, Sharon, then you should be practicing what you preach, and right now you are not."

"What are you talking about, Graham? I stand firm to my beliefs. I have never changed that! I've never compromised my beliefs, and I will not compromise myself, not even for my daughter."

"So it's a part of your belief then to still be in love with your dead husband so that even at night when you are lying beside me, your current husband, you're still calling Colton's name? Are you cheating on me or are you cheating on Colton? Because you are neither faithful to the living nor the dead!"

Shocked by the statement, Sharon looks at Graham. He has never spoken to her like that. "How are you speak to me like that! Have you lost your mind?"

"No, but keep this foolishness up, and I will lose my wife." Graham left Sharon openmouthed, staring after him.

Graham was right about her feelings for Colton. She loved Graham, but the love she shared with Colton was undeniably her greatest love. He was the love of her life.

Sharon had thought that secret was well-guarded in her heart, but obviously her dreams betrayed her. She still thinks of him every day, but in her heart, she knows that she is still upset with him.

She's had visions of their time together almost every night since he died. Colton abandoned her, and she blames him for going out to get the doll for Marissa that night. That one act forever changed their lives. If he had listened, he would still be here.

Sharon closes her eyes as the memory of the mangled wreck of Colton's car crushed underneath an oil tanker flashes across her mind.

Tears stream down her face. The last thing he said to her before he kissed her goodbye that night was that he would love her forever.

He broke that promise. Sharon now realizes that she has unknowingly resented Marissa. His love for her is why Colton went out that night and never returned. Sharon curls herself in a ball and sobs uncontrollably. Her very soul hurts.

She searches her mind for a prayer, a scripture, something to ease the pain that she has kept pent up for decades but came up empty. She wails even harder. "Lord, please help me," She sobs. That's all the prayer Sharon can muster.

Her relationship with her daughter is in ruins, and Colton, though dead, still torments her marriage with Graham. Sobs rocks her body even harder; she is the one who made this mess and knows she must be the one to fix it.

Just down the hall, Graham is in tears. Sharon's pain rips at his heart. Though it pains him to hear her wails, this time he decides he will not run to comfort her.

***

Inside the hospital room, Marissa gently cradles baby Jasmine to her as she nurses. Stephen sits next to the bed, lovingly looking on with a pleasant smile on his face. "How did I get so lucky?"

Marissa looks at him and smiles. "How did we get so lucky?" She kisses him. Baby Jasmine squirms. "I guess she doesn't like being squished," Marissa says, laughing. Stephen kisses her again and goes off to the bathroom.

Marissa reaches for the remote and flicks the TV on. On screen, Jason is finishing up another interview. She can't seem to escape him. It's like he is fated to invade her life once more on the day of his daughter's birth. She flicks to the next channel and yet again, there he is.

"Jason, what inspired your hit song 'Whisper in the Night?' And will you sing just a little for our audience today?" the host asks. Jason smiles. Instantly, Marissa remembers the first time he smiled at her in the car the night they met.

"Well…" Jason says, looking down at his rugged boots then smiling at the host, "sometimes you encounter people for brief moments in your life, and those moments are so precious and fleeting like a dream, almost like a whisper in the night. They disappear as quickly as they came, but their mark stains your soul for a lifetime." The host appears to be enthralled by him.

"Well, there you have it, ladies and gentlemen. Country music's newest heartthrob singing his latest hit, 'Whisper in the Night!'" The host walks over, hands the mic to Jason, and hugs him as he begins to sing.

"Cold and wet, I saw her standing, as beautiful as a dream.

Her smiles, her lips captivating, with eyes that still haunts my dreams…"

"Why is she acting like a lovestruck puppy?" Marissa wonders out loud. Stephen wheels in the room.

"Who is acting like a lovestruck puppy?" Stephen asks.

Startled, the remote falls from her hands. Her sudden movement wakes a sleeping Jasmine who now begins to cry. Marissa welcomes the sound of Jasmine's cries as she doesn't have a response for Stephen.

"Ummm, no one...can you turn the TV off for me please? She points to the remote on the ground, "I want to get her settled so that I can freshen up."

Stephen switches the TV off then motions to Marissa to give him the baby. Marissa watches as Stephen croons to little Jasmine.

"Te amo mi amor te amo eres hermosa mi amor, tan hermosa," Stephen sings. Guilt washes over Marissa. She now knows she was jealous of the woman for being so close to Jason.

***

Jasmine is settled in her crib. Soothing sounds of running water play from the sound machine. Marissa tiptoes out of her room and gently closes the door. Exhausted, she longs for a moment of quiet.

Since coming home from the hospital, the nights have been rough with Jasmine waking her up about every two hours, like a well-timed alarm clock, to feed.

"I'll listen for her," Cathryn says to Marissa. "Nathan and Stephen are putting up a swing and playhouse in the backyard."

Marissa smiles at Cathryn. "She isn't even ready for those yet," Marissa says, laughing, "but I know when Stephen and Nathan get something in their heads, there is no stopping them."

"Exactly," Cathryn says. "So let the boys be the boys. You go take a nap, a bath, a walk, whichever. Take some time for yourself. I have my granddaughter." Marissa hugs her mother-in-law.

Cathryn has been nothing but kind to her from the day they met. She wishes that her mother had some of Cathryn's traits. Sharon has not yet visited her granddaughter and Marissa wonders how long that will last.

"There is a bottle of freshly expressed breast milk in the fridge if she wakes. I could really use a long bath."

"You go right ahead, my love. I can take it from here." Cathryn kisses the top of Marissa's unkempt hair as Marissa thanks her.

The warmth of the bath calms Marissa. She relaxes her body as the soothing foam reaches all the way up to her neck. She reaches for her phone and opens to her music. She thinks of the song that Jason was singing when he was being interviewed.

Marissa wonders if the song was about her. Could she have affected his life so much that he wrote a song about her? Marissa finds herself typing in his name and looks at the many songs listed under his name. Her fingers hover over "*Whisper in the Night.*"

She twirls her hair deep in thought. "Do you wanna open that door, Marissa? And then what? So he wrote a song about you. Well, maybe he wrote a song about you. What are you gonna do? Call him up and say hey, Jason, I have a baby?...ummm..your baby?"

Marissa facepalms herself. "Girl, get your mind right and don't go looking for trouble." A part of her really wants to know what the rest of the song says, but she thinks better of it. She is a firm believer in leaving well enough alone.

Convinced that she has herself under control, she deletes Jason's name from the search. A few seconds later, the soothing sound of a female voice singing fills the room. Marissa relaxes, thinking to herself that this is a much safer choice.

She pushes the thought of Jason out of her mind and focuses her mind on what and who is important, Stephen and Jasmine.

***

Marissa and Stephen's backyard is filled with the sound of screaming children running and bouncing about and adults hanging out in little groups chatting. The banner on the wall reads HAPPY 1st BIRTHDAY, JASMINE.

Jade walks over with Jasmine to Marissa, who is busy restocking the table with snacks, while Natalia and Cathryn help her. "My niece is the smartest baby in the whole world! She just said Auntie Jade!" she exclaims with excitement.

"Jade, you know she did not," Natalia says, laughing. "Anyone's name she is going to call first is Auntie Nat."

"Well, I hate to burst both your bubbles. She's already called Stephen dad." She laughs at the disappointed looks on Natalia and Jade's faces. "Oh, and she can also say nan to Cathy as well."

"Oh, yes," Cathryn chimes in as Jasmine reaches for her.

"Nan," Jasmine says as if to show off her talking skills.

"Let's go check your bum quickly before it's time to blow out the candles on your cake," Cathryn says, kissing Jasmine. Jasmine giggles and holds on to her grandmother's face.

Graham walks in carrying huge gift-wrapped boxes. "There's my favorite girl."

"Oh, Daddy!" Marissa and Jade say mockingly. Graham looks at them and laughs.

"Oh no, not us?" they say, teasing.

Graham hugs his daughters, "You two are my favorite big girls." He takes the baby from Cathryn, but this little one is my favorite little girl." He kisses Jasmine's cheeks as she giggles happily. He hands her back to Cathryn, who disappears with her inside.

"So Mom is really missing her granddaughter's first birthday?" Marissa asks her dad.

Graham looks away as he sees the hurt in Marissa's eyes. "She was going to come, but just before I was ready to leave, she had a headache and went to take a nap."

"She could have taken an aspirin," Jade says sarcastically. "Dad, I love you, but you make too many excuses for Mom." She shakes her head at her dad. "I need a minute," she says, walking away.

"Issa, you know your mom. She'll come around," Graham says.

"Dad, Mom has only seen her grandchild twice since she was born! Once at her christening, and I figure she had no escape since it was being done at her church, and the second time at your birthday dinner. Again, no escape since it was at her house!" Marissa says, tears now filling her eyes.

Natalia consoles her. "Hey, Issa. It's okay." She hugs her friend. "No tears at my niece's party," she says, smiling at Marissa. "Come on, let's go check to see what kind of dress Cathryn is putting on her. I can' have my niece looking crazy on her birthday."

"I'm going to go find Stephen and Nathan. I know they are around here somewhere," Graham says, kissing Marissa. "I'm sorry, Peanut. I don't like to see you crying."

Marissa hugs her dad, "You've never made me cry, Daddy. In fact, you're always drying tears you have never caused." She kisses her dad. "I love you, Daddy."

"I love you too, Peanut," Graham says, blinking back tears.

"Softy," Jade whispers, just behind her dad. He laughs then hugs her too.

Marissa watches as Graham walks off to find Stephen and Nathan. She never knew what it felt like to not have a dad because Graham has been everything and more than she could ask for in a father. She silently thanks God for him.

Her mind trails to Stephen and Jasmine, and she silently prays that Stephen will love Jasmine unconditionally, the way Graham has loved her.

Later that night as Stephen and Marissa lay in bed, they listen to the sound of Jasmine gently breathing over the monitor. "I can't believe she's already one," Stephen says, "and she's so you, so full of life and so beautiful like her mom." Stephen kisses Marissa's hand.

Marissa smiles at Stephen, "I hope our relationship never becomes what mine and my mother's relationship is," Marissa says sadly.

"You're not your mom, Issa, and never will be," he reassures her. "I have a surprise for you. Well, it's kind of us." Stephen pulls himself up in bed and watches the delight on Marissa's face at the thought of a surprise.

"What is it?" Marissa asks eagerly.

"You're like a big kid," Stephen says, laughing. He hands Marissa an envelope. Marissa reads its content, "I think we could use a vacation as a family." Stephen says, looking at her.

"Oh babe, thank you! Yes! I need to clear my head, and this will be Jasmine's first trip out of the country! I am excited," Marissa says, bouncing on the bed all kid-like.

"It's settled then," Stephen says, laughing. "The first Paisley family vacation!" Marissa kisses him and rests her head on his chest. "And many more to come," he says as he kisses the top of her head.

"I love the sound of that," Marissa says. "Promise that you will love us forever?" Marissa asks, sleepily kissing his chest.

"To my last breath," he says, kissing her gently. "To my last dying breath." He listens to the rhythmical sound of her breathing as she nestles into him and falls asleep. In this still, silent moment, Stephen realizes that he is truly happier than he has been in ages.

***

The wide expanse of white sandy beach at the Silversands Beach Resort seems to stretch on for miles. Jasmine giggles happily, her wobbly feet racing to Stephen lying in the sand.

Marissa scoops her up just before she falls on Stephen. "Hand her over," Stephen demands, laughing. "I am very hungry. I am gonna eat her alive." Jasmine giggles even harder as Stephen pretends to eat her alive.

"Dada, Dada," Jasmine says between laughs. Stephen hugs his daughter and ruffles her curly brown hair. Marissa watches them and smiles. Stephen is happy. Jasmine has rekindled a light in his eyes that had vanished after his injuries.

She looks out over the turquoise blue water as surfers ride, inviting waves. She was happy. She had the family she always wanted. The man she loves is happy. Her daughter is happy. Everything about the day is perfect.

Marissa closes her eyes, and in her heart, she whispers a silent prayer of thanks to God. Against all odds, she and Stephen have weathered many storms and at the end of it all have truly been blessed.

"Happy?" Stephen asks.

"Immensely," Marissa replies, smiling at him.

"You both are my whole heart." Stephen says.

Marissa responds through tiny kisses on Stephen's face "And you both are mine." Stephen pulls her in closer and kisses her passionately. This time he did not pull away, instead he deepens the kiss, and Marissa feels hope mingled with sheer willpower in his kiss.

She is lost in him and he in her until Jasmine dumps sand from her little chubby hands on them, interrupting the intimate moment that they have not shared in forever.

Stephen grabs Jasmine and tickles her. Marissa smiles as she watches Stephen plays with his daughter. She feels hopeful that the intimacy they once shared will be rekindled. She is confident she felt hope in that kiss, and she feels hope in heart.

She closes her eyes and basks in the feelings, hoping that Stephen feels the same. She whispers a prayer as she has done many times before to God, holding on to hope for what was and what she believes still can be.

***

The dining room is filled with sunburnt tourists as Marissa wheels Stephen to their table. Jasmine bounces happily on his lap. "I'm gonna change her diaper. Order for me please and get her some mashed potatoes and carrots as well." Marissa kisses Stephen, takes a bouncing Jasmine off his lap, and heads toward the lobby.

Marissa searches through the baby bag on her shoulder as she heads to the restroom. She kisses the head of a squirming Jasmine. "Jas, I think I left your wipes in the room. Oops, I'm sorry." Marissa looks up to see who she has collided with. Shock registers on her face as she stares into familiar hazel-brown eyes. She knows these eyes very well. They are etched in her memory and ablaze with passion in her dreams.

He stoops down and gathers the items that fell from her bag. He looks at her then at Jasmine cooing happily in her arms. Recognition dawns on his face.

"Marissa?" He steps back in disbelief.

Marissa looks up at the ruggedly handsome man towering over her. Her breath catches in her throat. She feels woozy as if she is about to pass out. Maybe she raised her head too quickly just now, or maybe she was out in the sun too long.

Her world is suddenly spiraling out of control. The lobby walls look wobbly as if dancing. She is sure that any minute now she will hit the floor. She grips Jasmine as she feels Jason's arm steadying her. Marissa swoons against him. *I am dreaming.* Just then Jasmine's chubby little hands slap her cheeks excitedly.

"Mama, Mama." Jasmine coos. Marissa realizes she is definitely not dreaming. She also thinks she heard Jasmine say mama, but with all the thoughts running through her head, she could not be sure.

"Are you okay? It's Marissa, right?" Jason asks. Marissa stares at him blankly. *Maybe he won't recognize me if I don't say anything.*

"I know it's you. I can recognize your freckled face even in the thickest of crowds." He inches closer as if reading her thoughts. "It's this same face that has haunted my dreams for almost two years." It feels like Jason is incredibly close. Marissa cannot find the words to speak.

Jason hugs her. His hug was inviting, familiar, safe. Marissa forces herself to pull away.

A million things race through her mind. She looks up at Jason.

"Nothing to say from the girl who left a note that says I'm forever in her heart?"

Wow, he remembers. Her memory flashes back to that morning when she left him lying naked in bed asleep.

Even then Marissa knew that the connection between her and Jason was rare and long-lasting. Leaving him with just a note was one of the hardest things she had ever done.

Regardless of how Jason made her feel that night, her love for Stephen would not allow her to want anything more. Hurting Stephen was like hurting herself, and even though she often thought of Jason, she thought that he was safely tucked in the secret corners of her heart, never to be revealed.

Marissa pulls herself back to the present as she hears Jason talking to Jasmine. He is here now standing in front of her, guitar in hand, tattered jeans and T-shirt that he wears so well, and all the feelings of that night come flooding in.

Marissa feels the warmth creep to her cheeks, her hand instinctively touches her face as if to mask the evidence that it now so clearly displays.

"Hi, cuteness." Jasmine giggles at Jason. "And who is this little princess?" Jason asks. "Aren't you a little cutie?" He laughs at a bubbly Jasmine. "I think your mother can no longer speak." Marissa looks at him, secretly praying that Jason does not see the resemblance in Jasmine.

Jasmine is a constant reminder of Jason, from her inherited eyes to her smile. Though freckled like Marissa, she looks like Jason. Marissa knows this and prays Jason does not see it.

"Nice to see you again, Jason," Jason mimics, taking Marissa's hand. "I have thought of you as much as you have thought of me." Marissa hears the words coming out of Jason's mouth, but she still cannot find words of her own.

Jason takes her hand and gently brings it to his lips. Marissa watches as if in a dream. His lips graze gently across the back of her hand. She shudders.

Jason's eyes lock on hers knowingly. She is almost sure he feels her reaction to him because now he is incredibly close. He lingers over her hand and then leans in and kisses her cheeks.

Marissa awakens from the shock of seeing him and the closeness of him standing in front of her. Jasmine reaches for the toy hanging on her baby bag and Marissa finally musters every single ounce of strength in her body to pull away from him.

"Issa, you left Jas's wipes." Marissa froze as she heard Stephen's voice behind her. For a split second, she is confused. Jason watches as the blood drains from Marissa's face, and once again, his arm reaches out to steady her.

CHAPTER 8

"Marissa?" Stephen says.

She turns to Stephen, obviously flustered. "Wipes? Er...Oh yes, babe, thank you. I was searching for those."

"Is everything okay, Issa?" Stephen looks curiously at Jason. There is something familiar about the man that's standing just inches away from his wife and daughter. Marissa looks like she has seen a ghost of Christmas past.

Marissa's mind is racing. Any minute now she is gonna make a mess in her jeans. She looks at Stephen and knows his mind is working. She can see it on his face.

Mighty stars, Marissa thought, *maybe I should just faint. That would be better than standing here between both of them. Not a good plan,* she decides. *Jasmine would fall.* She definitely can't risk that.

"Wait a minute! I know you!" Stephen says, "Saunders, right? Private Saunders? Marissa's legs buckle, and Jason and Stephen instinctively reach out to steady her. "Sit, Issa." Both he and Jason guide her to a seat along the lobby wall. "Maybe you were out in the sun too long today?"

Marissa can't answer. Her throat is dry and itchy. Bile is sitting in her throat, and any minute now, she feels she is about to empty her insides on both of them. Her two planets are colliding, and she can do nothing about it.

Stephen lifts Jasmine off her lap. He looks at Marissa. She looks like a deer caught in headlights. "Issa, do you need me to get you some tea or something? Ginger ale?" Marissa shakes her head.

Stephen turns back to Jason. "You're Private Saunders, right? A little older, but I'm almost sure it's you."

Jason stares at Stephen. Recognition sets in as Jason thinks back to the day that Stephen saved his life. "Colonel Paisley?" Jason asks, looking curiously at Stephen then back at Marissa.

No, no, no, no, no! Marissa's mind screams. *What is happening? How do they know each other? This can't be happening!* Marissa clutches the baby bag. She needs to feel something beneath her fingers, otherwise she will think that this is a bad dream. *Of all the men on the planet, Marissa Swanson-Paisley, and you selected one that Stephen knows?* she asks herself then gasps, hoping she did not say that out loud. *Wake up, Marissa. Girl, you know you are not sleeping. I wish Jade or Nat were here. They would know what to say. Where is that dang phone a friend option when you need one?*

Marissa watches as Jason and Stephen greet each other. It's like she is watching from outside her body. Never in a million years did she ever think that something like this would happen. *I really thought I went far enough away and found someone that I wasn't likely to meet again.* Now he's on her TV and live, standing in front of her, talking to her husband. "Dang! He's everywhere."

"Who is everywhere?" Stephen asks, looking at Marissa, puzzled.

Dumb-dumb, yep, you said that out loud. While she searches for an answer for Stephen, she can feel both their eyes glued on her. She looks at Jason; he has a sly grin on his face. Her mind is blank. She has nothing. Jade would come in handy at this moment. She is the queen of quick comebacks.

"Yes, Stephen Paisley." Stephen extends his hand to Jason, and they shake hands. "How do you two know each other?" Stephen asks, looking from Marissa to Jason. Jason gazes at his shoes then glances at Marissa.

Marissa looks pleadingly at Stephen, who waits for an answer. Neither of them responds.

"Saunders, this is my wife, Marissa. Marissa...Saunders, but I believe you two know each other already."

Stephen looks at his wife. Her face is panicked. Jasmine coos on his lap. "And this is our daughter Jasmine," Stephen says, kissing a gurgling Jasmine.

Jason looks at the baby then at Marissa and Stephen and back at Jasmine. Now he is the one weak in the knees, about to pass out. He leans against the wall. The guitar in his hands slips from him. He looks at Marissa questioningly. "How old is she?" he asks Stephen, his eyes never leaving Marissa.

"Thirteen months," Stephen says, intently watching Marissa and Jason.

Marissa knows that Jason knows, and she knows that Jason knows that she knows he knows. She also knows that Stephen knows, and all Marissa can think about is to grab her baby and run. She can't think of any other scenario where this ends well. She needs to go, and she needs to go now.

"Babe, I'm not feeling well. Can we go back to the room?" Marissa asks.

Jason walks over to Stephen. "Sir, you saved my life that day, and I did not get a chance to say thank you." He looks down at Stephen's legs. "I owe you a lot." Jason extends his hand to Stephen, and Stephen shakes it.

"We should have a drink," Stephen says. "How long are you here for?" Marissa looks at Stephen horrified. Stephen holds her gaze.

"My show is tonight. I'm free in another two hours." He looks at Marissa and Stephen then at Jasmine. "Actually, I have time now for a quick drink." He looks at Marissa as if daring her to object.

"Issa, are you up for a drink?" Stephen asks. Marissa shrugs her shoulders, feeling trapped.

Stephen wheels ahead with a giggling Jasmine. Marissa follows behind with Jason next to her. She can feel his eyes piercing into her. "Marissa," Jason says. Her name is like a whisper on his lips, but she hears it.

She looks at him, "Yes?"

"How long have you been married?" Jason asks her. Marissa knew where he was going with the conversation.

"Yes, Jason, I was married the night I was with you."

"So you just decided to go out and cheat on your husband? Not only that, you cheated on your husband with me? The man who…." Jason's voice trails off as he looks at her in disbelief.

"You don't understand what you're talking about," Marissa says to him.

"Then make me understand, Marissa!" He reaches out and holds her hand, stopping her from walking. Marissa watches as Stephen and Jasmine disappear around the corner. "We shared one unforgettable night, well for me at least, then you up and disappear, and two years later, here you are with a baby and the man who saved my life! Help me to understand, Marissa, because I really don't."

"The scars," Marissa says, remembering the scars along his abdomen and his hip, "that's where you got those scars."

"Yes," Jason says, "your husband used his body as a human shield for me and a little girl. I am alive today because of his sacrifice. I didn't even know he made it because he was badly injured." Jason's voice trails off as if he is reliving the moment.

"Stephen doesn't talk much about that day." Marissa says to Jason. "It stole a lot from him, from us."

"Marissa, you're his wife and I slept with you, and I've thought about you night and day since then."

"I have thought about you too, Jason. It wasn't just one night for me." Marissa hears what she is admitting openly. "I can't do this, Jason. I love Stephen. What we shared was one night." She pulls her hand away and starts hurrying after Stephen and Jasmine.

Jason catches up to her. "One night and a child?" Jason asks but with certainty. Marissa stops and stares at him then shakes her head.

"You don't understand."

"You've said that already, Marissa, yet you still haven't made any effort to make me understand. And don't start denying that the child is mine. I can recognize my own face and eyes. As a matter of fact, they are my mother's eyes. She even has her name."

"Your mom's name is Jasmine?" Marissa asks in disbelief.

"Yes, Jasmine Saunders. She's been gone over four years now," Jason says sadly. "What are the odds?"

Really what are the odds? Marissa, it just gets better and better with you. Jade and Nat are gonna have a field day with this. Jade probably will have som explanation about the stars being cosmically aligned. I this case, I wish they were cosmically aligned somewhere else.

***

Stephen, Jason, and Marissa are seated at the table, and baby Jasmine is in her highchair. Stephen turns to Jason. "So what have you been up to? When did you finish your tour?"

"Three years ago," Jason responds.

"From the army to music," Stephen muses.

"Something like that," Jason responds.

Stephen downs is drink in one gulp. "Listen, let's cut to the chase here. I know you believe my wife cheated on me with you, but I am here to tell you that's not the case."

Marissa and Jason are shocked at the directness of Stephen. "What, you two believe I don't know?" Stephen asks them, "I finally see where my daughter gets her hazel-brown eyes," he says, ruffling Jasmine's curls. Jason looks down at his feet while Marissa shifts uncomfortably in her chair.

"Da da," Jasmine says, grabbing her father's hand, bringing it to her mouth.

"If it wasn't you, it would have been some other random stranger, so don't leave here thinking it was anything special." Marissa is flabbergasted at how callously Stephen portrays her time with Jason.

"My only question is," Stephen continued, "now that you know, what's your intent?"

"Stephen Paisley!" Marissa says, getting up from the table. "What has gotten into you! You sound as if Jasmine and I are some property that you can auction off!" Marissa unbuckles Jasmine from her highchair.

"Say night-night to Daddy, Jas," Marissa says, leaning over so Jasmine can kiss her dad. "Say night-night to the nice gentleman." Jasmine waves bye-bye to Jason, who is still in shock at what just took place.

"We are finished here, Saunders!" Stephen says to Jason in a commanding tone before wheeling to follow Marissa. Jason sits, still too much in shock to move.

As Marissa boards the elevator, she sees that Stephen is right behind her. Marissa wants to be alone but holds the door open so that Stephen can enter. "I'm sorry," Stephen says as he enters. "I wasn't trying to…"

"Sorry?" Marissa says angrily. "Sorry, Stephen? What was that? You humiliated me. How could you treat me like that, Stephen? You sat there, and you treated me like crap."

"Issa, that was never my intent. You know that. What are you really angry about?"

"I said to you that I wasn't feeling well. That was our exit, but no, you had to stay. You wanted to exert your manliness but at my and Jas's expense."

Jasmine starts to fuss in Marissa's hand, and Marissa does her best to calm the anger that is coursing through her veins. "You weren't thinking about Jas and me with that display just now. You just wanted to get back at the man who made love to your wife."

"I thought you said it was nothing." Stephen stares at her. "So you made love now?"

"Don't twist my words, Stephen. You know exactly what I mean." Marissa looks away from Stephen's prying eyes. "You jeopardized Jas and me tonight, Stephen. That's what you did. As a matter of fact, I think we should just get our things and head to the airport."

Just then a family of four enters the elevator with the kids chatting up a storm. Stephen and Marissa scowl at each other from opposite ends of the elevator. Marissa does her best to hold it together because a fountain of tears is waiting to unleash any second now. The elevator gets to their floor and Stephen opens their room door.

"Marissa," Stephen says. Marissa picks up on the use of her full name. Stephen has called her that but only a few times in their ten years of marriage.

"I need to get Jas cleaned up and ready for bed," Marissa says, walking off before Stephen could say what he had to say.

"Marissa, we have to talk about this," Stephen calls after her.

Oh, so this is a habit now. Marissa says to herself. She realizes how much being called Issa by Stephen meant to her.

Marissa fills the bath while holding back her tears. She undresses Jasmine in silence while Jasmine bounces about, her usual happy self. A range of emotions—anger, sadness, self-pity—is going through her.

She watches as Jasmine playfully tries to squish the bubbles between her chubby little fingers. Marissa studies her daughter. She realizes in that moment, despite the turmoil now brewing between her and Jason and Stephen, she would endure it all and do it all over again just to meet the precious blessing that Jasmine is. Marissa kisses her bubbles-filled hair as she pulls her from the bath.

Marissa enters the bedroom of the hotel and looks around; she realizes that Stephen is gone. She towel dries Jasmine and feeds her a bottle.

Now comfortably resting in her mother's arms, Jasmine looks up at Marissa and says, "Mama." Marissa smiles at Jasmine.

Finally, she is saying mama. Marissa muses on the fact that the day was perfect with the intimate moment she shared with Stephen on the beach. Then hell broke loose when she ran into Jason, but somehow hearing Jasmine saying "mama" makes it all worth it.

She watches as Jasmine drifts off to sleep. The fountain waiting patiently behind her eyes for a while now finally gives way and comes cascading down her face.

Marissa wishes that Stephen was in the room even though they were fighting. Jasmine has finally said "mama," and Stephen wasn't here to hear it. *What a mess this is.* Her mom would have a field day with this if she knew how Marissa's life was unraveling.

Marissa kisses the top of Jasmine's head. The smell of shea butter conditioner still lingers in her hair. She cradles her daughter close, and like Jasmine, she too drifts off to sleep.

***

Stephen enters the room to find Marissa and Jasmine sleeping; it is one of the most beautiful sights that he has ever seen. Marissa is even more beautiful a a mother. The love he feels for them is fierce and protective, and he will battle to his last breath to keep them happy and protected. Stephen knows that Jason will not just disappear.

From the determination Jason showed in removing the bomb from the little girl that fateful day, Stephen knows he isn't the type to give up. *But neither am I the type to give up or walk away. I will do everything in my power to ensure that my family remains safe and intact even if it costs me my life.* Stephen kisses Marissa's head. He remembers their moment on the beach earlier. How he misses being with her in that way.

He would give almost anything to once more make love to his wife and have her all spent and satisfied looking up at him.

He thought of Saunders. Now there is a face to the stranger who has haunted his thoughts and his dreams since the day Marissa came back home.

Stephen now realizes that the feeling that he has not been able to shake since she returned was not jealousy, but rather fear. Fear of losing the woman he loves and now the daughter that he loves.

***

Jason's mind is a mangled mess as he thought of his encounter with Marissa and Colonel Paisley. He has tried to block out the fateful day in Iraq. It is too painful to revisit. Yet with Colonel Paisley here, he can't help but go back.

He thought Colonel Paisley died that day. No way could he have survived a blast that ripped his legs off and tore through his lower abdomen.

As bloodied as Jason was that day, during bouts of consciousness when he looked over at Colonel Paisley's remains, he was sure he was dead. Pieces of him were scattered across the ground. It is a miracle that he made it.

Jason is fully aware that he owes him his life. He mulls over what Colonel Paisley meant by "If it was not him it would have been any random stranger."

The knock on his door brings him back to the present. It was time to take the stage. For once in his life, Jason feels no joy to go on stage to sing. He wants nothing more than to go to Marissa, to talk to her, to touch her, to kiss her once more.

On stage, Jason is closing out his set. His closing song is usually his hit song *"Whisper in the Night."* The words are coming from Jason's lips, but his mind is elsewhere.

He looks out at the screaming crowd, but all he sees are flashbacks of a mesmerizing Marissa lying beneath him to the scared, frightened woman he saw earlier. In that moment he wanted to just pull her close to him and assure her that she was safe.

Then his mind goes to Jasmine. Her smile has already stolen his heart. He knows he loves and wants her. He knows he can't exist in a world where he is not a part of Jasmine's life.

He questions if those feelings are actually for Jasmine or Marissa, but he knows it is about Jasmine. He has a daughter and intends to be a part of her life even if it costs him every penny that he has.

***

Sunlight streams through the partially drawn curtain of the hotel room. Marissa wakes to see Jasmine snuggled in-between her and Stephen. She watches them for a bit. These are the two most important people to her on the face of this earth, and as mad as she is at Stephen presently, he is the love of her life. She will protect that love as fiercely as a mama bear protects her cub. Marissa dresses, ties the laces of her sneakers, and quietly exits.

A vigorous run usually clears Marissa's head and helps her to think clearly. She thinks about her mother and wishes that she could call her at this very moment, but Marissa knows that judgment will follow, so she quickly dismisses that thought from her head.

She thinks better of Jade and Natalia. Jade will go instantly into fight mode, and Natalia will go into lawyer mode. Marissa runs even harder. This is a problem she is going to have to solve on her own.

She pushes herself to the limit, barely noticing the runners on the trail with her. She just wants to go as hard and as fast as she can. Maybe she can outrun her troubles.

Daddy, maybe Daddy, she thought, *he's such a wise old soul.* Marissa smiles at the thought of her dad. He has talked her out of many ruts before. She figures in this situation he will know exactly what to do, minus the judgment. Marissa settles on that in her mind and finally starts observing the beauty of her surroundings.

From the running trail, Marissa sees the waves from the beach racing to greet the shoreline. Early morning surfers are already out taking advantage of the eager waves, and a few people are either walking or running along the beach.

She thinks of Jason and the hurt and shock on his face last night. She cares deeply for him and does not want to hurt him either. His world is also now turned upside down, and she is responsible for that. The realization that there is no easy fix to this situation dawns on her.

"Marissa!" She stops abruptly in her tracks, and the runner behind her almost collides into her.

"Sorry!" Marissa calls out in apology as the woman runs past her. Marissa crosses the street. Jason is dripping with sweat, his arms bulging from the sleeveless tank that he is wearing.

"You're a jogger too," he says, half-smiling at her, "and little by little the mystery that is Marissa Paisley is unfolding. I thought you said that there were no layers to you."

Marissa drinks him in, the incredible sculpted beauty of him is mind-altering "What you see is what you get. Now there's a big fat lie," Jason says somewhat sarcastically.

"Where's your wife or girlfriend, Jason? Do you have one of those?" Marissa wonders why she asked the question because it really had no relevance. "Correction. Girlfriends, groupies, whatever you famous people have?"

Jason grins at her. "Unlike you, I do not have any significant other lurking in the shadows, and literally, what you see is what you get with me."

Marissa looks up at him, still catching her breath, "What about kids?" Again, she wonders where this line of questioning is going. She convinces herself that the more she knows about him the more ammunition she will have should a battle ensue.

Jason looks at her, his eyebrows raised, "One," he responds.

"Okay," Marissa says, still looking at him.
That's good. He has a child so he will not want mine.

"I met her last night," Jason continues, watching as her face goes motionless for a split second. He recognizes the fear in her eyes. It pains him. He would rather have her looking at him with intense passion like the night they met than with fear or pain.

"I gotta go." Marissa says, but Jason blocks her path.

"You're not running off like you did last night. Is this how you live your life? By running each chance you get?"

"Jason, move," she says, pleading. "I have to get back to Stephen and Ja…," her voice trails off.

"Jasmine? Our daughter?" Jason finishes for her. "Marissa, what kind of man do you think I am? Do you think I am just going to disappear, knowing that I have a child out there?"

"Jasmine is mine and Stephen's child!" Marissa lashes out.

"Oh, so a paternity test then?" Jason asks her.

"You know what I mean!"

"Actually, I don't! I don't, Marissa! You got in my car and then into my bed! You now have my child and expect that I should just turn and walk away and say what? Have a good life?" Marissa looks away from Jason. His eyes change color when he gets angry.

Focus, Marissa tells herself.

"Jason, my intent was never to hurt you. What we shared was supposed to be one night. I had no clue I would ever meet you again, and I sure did not know who you were until your face popped up on the screen one day. I don't want anything from you. I wasn't trying to get pregnant to stick you with a baby for money."

"Your intent was to get pregnant though! Marissa, you used me. I was simply a sperm donor to you!"

"It wasn't like that! You're not hearing me."

"What exactly am I not hearing?" Jason asked.

"It was only supposed to be one night, Jason! Yes, I wanted a baby, and yes, I may have used you for that, but you and I share a connection that I can't deny. Whether or not I was trying to make a baby, I would have still made love to you." Marissa shocked herself with that confession, even though she knew from the beginning that Jason was more than one night. To deny that would be lying to herself.

"So I should be honored that you chose me to father your child? Is that what I hear?" Jason asked.

"You are twisting everything I say. I'm done talking. Like I said, Jas is mine and Stephen's child. That's it."

"You're missing the point, Marissa," Jason says, reaching for her hands. "You have a baby, my baby. It's no longer one night as you poetically put it, and now that I know, I will not walk away."

Marissa yanks her hands away. "Like I said, I have to get back."

Jason steps out of her way, "You can go, Marissa, but this is not over." Marissa starts running. "And you can run like you did the last time, but this time I will find you, Marissa Paisley!" He calls after her.

Marissa ignores him and keeps running. Sweat drips from Marissa as she enters the hotel room. Stephen is up, feeding Jasmine. Marissa walks over and kisses her hair. "I'm gonna call the airline and see if we can get a flight out. I have to get back," Marissa says to Stephen.

"I'm not running, Marissa, if that's your though here. I am not running," Stephen says firmly.

"Okay, then Jas and I will leave."

"And then what? Look over your shoulders for the rest of your life, wondering if he's gonna show up? What happened this morning? Were you with him?" Stephen's tone is almost accusatory.

"I was not with him, with him." Marissa replies. "I went for a run and ran into him."

"You two sure run into each other often," Stephen says sarcastically.

"I don't care to know what you're implying, Stephen, but one thing I know is that I'm not doing this with you. I am not gonna stand here and have you accuse me of cheating. I have never cheated on you! Never!"

"Really?" Stephen says. "Then how did we get here?"

Marissa stares at Stephen in shock and utter disbelief. She heads to the bathroom and slams the door.

***

Jason paces back and forth in his hotel room. He is furious about how the conversation with Marissa went. That was not his plan. The last thing he wants to do is hurt her. The scared look on her face guts him.

Many times he has fantasized about seeing her again, and the scared look on her face was never what he imagined. He knows he messed up and he intends to fix it. There must be an amicable way that they can all coparent Jasmine.

Jason is confident he can put his feelings for Marissa aside and concentrate on being a part of his daughter's life. That's what is most important here.

He picks up the phone and rings the front desk. This time he knows Marissa's name. "Marissa and Stephen Paisley's room please?" He listens intently as the receptionist clicks on the keyboard. He takes a deep breath as he tries to formulate what he will say to them.

"I am sorry, but those guests have already checked out," the receptionist says.

"Are you sure? Can you try their room, please?" Jason replies.

"I'm sure," the receptionist says, "I called a car to take them to the airport earlier."

"Thank you," Jason says as he hangs up the phone. He shakes his head in disbelief. "So you ran again, Marissa." He says out loud, "But this time I will follow you to the ends of the earth. You can count on that!"

CHAPTER 9

The airplane ride back home is silent aside from Jasmine's giggles and usual baby chatter. Neither Marissa nor Stephen speak a word to each other.

Marissa's gut tells her that Jason is not the type to disappear now that he knows he has a child. She just needs to get home so that she can clearly think what her next move will be.

She makes a mental note to call Natalia. If there is anyone who will know some way to get her out of this legally, Natalia will know what it is.

From the car, Marissa calls Cathryn. "Cathy, are you up for some sloppy kisses today? I have some errands to run," Marissa asks.

"Anytime," Cathryn says excitedly.

"Okay, we are headed to you," Marissa says, hanging up the phone.

"So I can't watch our daughter now?" Stephen asked.

"Stephen, please don't start. I don't think I have much fight left in me. Furthermore, we have exposed Jas to a lot of negative tension this weekend. It stops today. My sole responsibility is to protect her. She's my first priority."

Stephen is about to respond, but when he sees the look on his wife's face, he decides not to.

Nathan is headed through the door, briefcase in hand, when Marissa and Stephen pull in. He rests the briefcase at the door and takes his granddaughter. "Hello, my beautiful princess. You're nicely tanned." Jasmine giggles and pulls at his beard. "I missed my little princess," he says, tickling her as Jasmine giggles even harder.

"Give me my grandbaby," Cathryn says, plucking Jasmine from Nathan's hand. "Look! You've grown this much." Cathryn extends her hand showing Jasmine how much she has grown, and Jasmine laughs with her grandmother. "Say bye-bye to pop-paw. He has to run." Nathan leans in for one of Jasmine's sloppy kisses.

"Will you be in the office today?" Nathan asks Marissa.

"Probably later in the evening. I have some errands to run." She hugs her father-in-law.

"Walk me out, son." Nathan motions to Stephen, and Stephen obliges.

Nathan waits until they are at the car, and then he turns to his son. "What's going on with you and Marissa? I sensed some tension."

"Dad, everything is a mess. I said some things, she said some things, and I just don't know."

"Son, listen. You and Marissa have been through some rough times. She stayed at your bedside night and day nursing you back to health. She loves you and I know you love her. Fix it. Life is too precious.

You have a beautiful daughter who needs both her parents, so work it out." Nathan's warning is stern. Stephen feels like he is ten all over again, and his dad is scolding him for getting in a fight at school.

Nathan hugs his son, then looks at him. "I know the man you are, so I know you will make this right." With that, he jumps into his truck and is gone.

Before Stephen makes his way back in the house, Marissa is on her way out. "Do you need me to drop you at home? I have to run out after." Stephen nods and follows Marissa to the car. "Your mom says that she will call you later. She's gonna try to get Jas down for a nap." Stephen nods in response.

They drive in silence for a while, and even though he thinks better of it, he still has to ask. "Why did you drop Jas to my mom? Do you think I am incapable of watching her?" he asks Marissa.

"Are you really asking me this, Stephen?" Marissa says in a resigned tone. "I thought we could both use a break; I have errands to run, and I didn't want to saddle you with Jas."

"There it is." Stephen says to Marissa, disappointment evident in his voice, "Saddle? When has my daughter ever been a burden to me?" Stephen shakes his head. "Marissa, are you hearing what you are saying? You called my mom to watch our daughter without even asking me?"

So I'm still Marissa, she muses to herself. "You're picking a fight, Stephen, and I'm not in the mood to fight with you. Everything I say you twist it. I am done fighting."

"Answer me this," Stephen says, "tell me that you don't have feelings for Saunders. I saw the way you were when he kissed you last night. Tell me I am wrong."

Marissa was secretly hoping that Stephen had not seen that exchange between her and Jason. She tries hard to think about how to respond.

"I was shocked! I never expected to ever see im again! How did you want me to respond?" Marissa lares at Stephen angrily.

"Marissa, I know you, and I know what I saw."

"Why the bloody hell do you keep calling me Marissa! You've not called me that in ages!"

"Don't try and change the subject, Mar…. Issa." Stephen says. "Do you have feelings for him or not?"

Marissa looks at him, "I don't know what you hought you saw, but I already answered the question, nd I will not sit here and allow you to accuse me of heating on you like you did this morning."

"I never accused you of cheating."

"You implied it! You're acting like I'm some vhore who stepped out on her husband! You made this lecision with me! If anyone cheated, you did! You ran)ack to Iraq a few days after we got married! You got njured! Our sex life ended! And then you basically)awned me off to the first stranger who could do what ou couldn't! That's on you, Stephen! If anyone heated, you should first look in the mirror!"

Marissa continues her rant, "What is bothering you is the fact that you want to know if I enjoyed it! That's what is eating away at you! We have been sidestepping that question for some time now! Yes, I enjoyed it! I am a young woman with red blood coursing through my veins! I enjoyed it! I wanted it! There! I have said what you wanted me to say the minute I came home two years ago! I hope that makes you feel better! Yes, I cheated on you with your permission! There! I have said it all! Now what?"

The rage Marissa feels is new to her. Even though she sees the pained look on Stephen's face as the words pour like venom from her lips, she can't stop herself.

At this moment, she wants to hurt him. She wants him to feel exactly what she is feeling. The look on his face says that she is successful.

"Issa, look out!" Stephen yells. "Look out!"

Marissa sees the horror on Stephen's face and turns her attention back to the road. She hears her own screams echo in her ears before the sound of crunching metal colliding against metal. The SUV skids for what seems like miles as the semi-truck screeches to a smoking halt.

"Stephen! Stephen!" Marissa screams, reaching over, trying to get to him. The death grip of the seat belt is tight around her chest, and Marissa feels like she can't breathe.

Blood pools down from Stephen's head, painting a red pathway down his face. Marissa follows the trail of blood streaming down Stephen's face.

Stephen is not moving. She reaches for him. She needs to touch him. "Please be okay, Stephen." Marissa whispers, "Please, babe, be okay. I love you." There is soggy wetness at the back of her neck. Marissa's hand touches it. She is bleeding, and heavily, she guesses. She can feel it running down the back of her shirt.

This can't be how our life ends. This is not how our chapter ends. Marissa looks over at a motionless Stephen. She thinks of Jasmine's beautiful face, her giggles, and sloppy kisses. *No, this is not how it ends.*

Her mind travels to Stephen, to their wedding day, the happiness of that moment. She thinks of her mom. Sharon would be praying in this situation. Marissa tries to pray but doesn't know where to begin.

Somewhere in the bundle of floating memories, Jason's face creeps in. Marissa struggles to hold onto consciousness, but a dark abyss beckons to her. Marissa reluctantly gives in as the blackness seeps in.

***

Marissa wakes to a blinding white light immediate panic sets in. *Am I dead? Is this the heaven Mom is always talking about? Is my soul traveling? Jasmine!* Her mind screams, *No, I have to be here for Jasmine!*

Marissa tosses and frays about. She hears sounds from a distance away. She feels trapped like she cannot move. *What's happening?* her mind screams.

"Mrs. Paisley! Mrs. Paisley! Can you hear me? Follow my finger if you can?" Marissa tried her best to focus, but the light was so bright. "Mrs. Paisley, I'm Dr. Cranston. Can you hear me?"

Hospital? I am in the hospital! Marissa's mind screams. Joy creeps in. *I'm in the hospital. That means...that means..."* Marissa's mind finally wakes up and she finds her speech.

"Jasmine!" she screams.

"Who is Jasmine?" Marissa hears the doctor ask.

"Jasmine is her daughter," Sharon responds.

"Mom? Mom?" Marissa's eyes pop open. She tries to sit up.

"No, no, no." Dr. Cranston says, "Don't! Don't try to sit up."

"I'm here, darling." Sharon says.

Oh Lord! This has to be bad! "Mom is here? Am I dying?" Marissa asks, her eyes focusing on the blond-haired doctor looming over her. He barely looks a day over twenty.

"Yes," the doctor responds.

"Yes, I'm dying?" Marissa asked.

"No," the doctor grins sheepishly. "No, you're not dying. Yes, your mom is here."

Marissa looks past the doctor to see her mom, a worried look on her face. "Mom, oh, Mom," Marissa sobs. Sharon hugs her daughter as sobs rock her body. "Mom, it was pretty bad, Mom. Stephen? Where is Stephen?" Memories of the accident comes flooding back.

"Your husband is still in surgery." Dr. Cranston says. "He sustained some head injuries, and they are operating currently."

"Will he be okay?" Marissa cries.

Sharon motions to the doctor not to respond. Marissa catches the exchange. If anything happens to Stephen, Marissa is not sure how she will live with herself.

"Marissa, darling, just stay calm. Nathan promises to update me as soon as he's out of surgery," Sharon consoles her daughter. "Now I need you to relax and not exert yourself too much. You have a nasty gash on the back of your head, but the doctor has stitched it up nicely."

Marissa's hand instinctively went to the back of her head. Her fingers traced over the length of the gauze taped to her head.

"Where's Jasmine?"

"Cathryn took her home; the little cuteness was exhausted. We thought it was best to get her home and away from the hospital craziness. I told Cathryn to call when she gets home, so now that you're awake I'm sure you can video call her." Sharon's voice is sweet and soothing. Marissa feels as if she is in a dream.

She's too sweet for me not to be dying. I don't think they're telling me the truth.

"Your dad, Jade, and Natalia are in the waiting room. Only one of us is allowed in at a time."

"And you came?" Marissa asks her mom.

"Do you want me to leave?" Sharon asks sadly. 'I don't want to upset you."

"No, Mom, I don't want you to leave. I'm just surprised, that's all. I'm glad you are here." Marissa reaches for her mother's hand. "Will you sing to me?"

Sharon's voice cracks, "What do you want me to sing?" she asks gently, stroking Marissa's hair.

"His Eye is on the Sparrow," Marissa says, smiling weakly. Marissa remembers falling asleep to her mom singing that song to her many times. Tears sting the corner of her eyes. They have lost so much over the years. Marissa makes a mental note to work harder at her and her mom's relationship.

She closes her eyes as she listens to the soothing sound of her mother's golden voice singing. Its familiarity relaxes her. She would like Jasmine to have that experience of her Grandma Sharon singing to her. Between the tears and the exhaustion that Marissa feels, she soon drifts off to sleep.

***

"Mom?" Marissa blinks, not sure what time it is. "Mom?"

"Issa, it's me. It's Nat." Natalia holds her friend's hand.

"Nat, what time is it? Where is Mom? Did Cathy call?"

"Issa, you had a concussion. You have been sleeping for the past three days. Sharon went home just a few hours ago to take a shower. Jade and Graham literally had to drag her from your bedside. She's really worried about you."

Marissa tries to sit up in bed. "Take it easy, Issa. Let me help you." Natalia helps Marissa to a seated position in the bed. Marissa looks around the room. "Jas and Cathy are fine. Sharon gave Cathy strict orders to keep Jas out of the hospital until…" Natalia's voice trails off.

"Until what, Nat? What are you not telling me?"

"Nothing," Nat responded, "She just wanted to make sure that you and Stephen are okay."

"Stephen? Where is Stephen?" Is he okay?

"Yes, he'll be okay. As soon as the nurse returns, I'll find out if you can see him. He is in the ICU."

Marissa tears up. "I caused this, Nat. I did. We were arguing and then the next thing I know there is a semi coming directly at us. There was so much blood. Stephen wasn't moving. It was pretty bad." Marissa sobs uncontrollably.

"Issa, you have to stay calm. It wasn't your fault. Stephen is fine. I saw him, and we spoke. He'll be fine. He is worried out of his mind and just wants you to be okay," Natalia says.

"I was gonna drop him home and come to see you. I needed some legal advice regarding Jason. We ran into him at the resort. He knows, Nat." Marissa says, looking worriedly at her friend. "He knows, and I don't think he is gonna just go away."

"I know. Stephen told me. Like I told him, we just have to wait and see if he makes any move. For all we know, he may just forget about you and Jasmine."

"He won't forget, Nat. He's not the forgetting type. We shouldn't have gone on that vacation. Everything has gone wrong since then." Marissa hides her face under the covers.

"Issa, you have one of the best defense attorneys on the planet. Jason and what army can come for you?"

Marissa smiles at Natalia's warrior stance. Just then the nurse enters, and Natalia makes arrangements for them to go to Stephen's room.

Natalia's phone rings and she answers. It's Cathy on video call. Natalia watches as her friend's face lights up with the joy of seeing Jasmine bubbly and giggly on camera.

"Oh, Cathy, thank you for taking care of Jas. I'm so sorry this happened," Marissa says to Cathryn.

"Oh, hush, child. Just get better and come on home. You scared us there for a minute, but my grandbaby is in good hands. She's being spoiled rotten."

"That's what I'm afraid of." Marissa and Natalia laugh.

*   *   *

Inside the ICU, it is bone-chilling cold. Marissa shivers as the cold penetrates the hospital gown she's wearing. Nathan sees her and gets up from Stephen's bedside. He hugs Marissa. "I am glad to see you awake. Don't scare me like that again." He hugs her tighter.

He motions to Natalia that he will take control of her wheelchair, and he wheels Marissa over to Stephen's bedside.

Marissa is shocked at the sight of Stephen. He is completely bald, and three rows of staples cover his head like a train track. Marissa gasps and the tears start to flow. "Issa, please, don't cry. I'm fine. Just a few scrapes and bruises. Nothing I'm not used to," he jokes.

"Babe, I'm so sorry…"

"Shhh," Stephen says, "there's nothing to be sorry about. None of this is your fault. I'm just glad you're okay. How is Jas? I don't want her to see me on camera like this, so I haven't video called her yet."

"She's fine. She looks so big. Cathy video called me earlier, and she was chatting up a storm with me."

"Cat is spoiling her rotten. I can tell you that much," Nathan said, laughing. "I'm going to run home and check on them. I'll see you later, son." Nathan kisses Stephen's head and then kisses Marissa's cheek. "I'll see you soon, Marissa."

He waves goodbye to Natalia. "Thank you for being here," he says, smiling at her. Natalia smiles at Nathan. Marissa watches as her father-in-law exits. She senses a change in him but is not sure what it is.

Stephen reaches for her hand. He brings it to his lips. "I missed you. I thought I lost you there for a minute." He looks at her, "No more fighting. Whatever happens, we will face it head-on, together."

"Together," Marissa says, leaning over to kiss him.

Natalia watches the exchange between them with a hint of sadness, but mostly joy that they share such pure and genuine love for each other. She was happy that if she did not have Stephen's heart at least her best friend and sister does.

"I can't wait to be home in our bed with you. My old bones are aching from this bed." Stephen laughs. His laugh is warm and refreshing and reaches his eyes. Marissa is happy to see that smile. She missed it and she missed him.

Natalia gets up to leave just as Dr. Cranston walks in, his stethoscope hanging around his neck and a folder in his hand. He smiles as he sees Marissa. "It's good to see you up and about, Mrs. Paisley." Dr. Cranston extends his hand to greet her.

"Likewise, Doctor...Doctor" Marissa says, searching for his name.

"Cranston," he says with a quirky smile. Marissa laughs inwardly. He was such a nerdy young man.

"So good news, Mr. Paisley." Stephen looks at him expectantly, "You should be going home in a few days. However, you will need to be back here so that we can start your…"

"That's great news, Dr. Cranston." Stephen cut him off abruptly. "I was just telling my wife that my old bones need my own bed."

"What will he need to come back for, doctor?" Marissa asked. Stephen gives Dr. Cranston a warning look, and he refrains from answering.

"Just a regular checkup and to remove these staples," Stephen kisses Marissa's hand, reassuring her. "Can't have me going around looking like a gargoyle."

"You're really getting old," Marissa says, laughing.

"I'll make my rounds, and I'll check back in on you before I leave," Dr. Cranston says.

The nurse returns to take Marissa back to her room. Natalia kisses her friend and hugs Stephen and exits.

Marissa kisses her husband goodbye and hugs him tightly; she feels so fragile in his arms. He holds her closer. All he has ever wanted is to love and protec her. Stephen reluctantly lets her go as she kisses him one final time.

Dr. Cranston walks over as soon as Marissa exits. "Mr. Paisley, you really should tell your wife about your diagnosis. You don't have a lot of time, fiv to six months at most. You will need all the support you can get."

"Dr. Cranston, I appreciate your medical opinion, but I haven't seen my wife's smile in many days. I was not going to erase it by telling her that I have glioblastoma with only a few months left to live."

Stephen looks at the disapproval on Dr. Cranston's face. "I know what's best for my wife, and now was not the time to tell her. But I will tell her when I think she can handle it."

***

The front door to Marissa and Stephen's home opens just as Nathan's van pulls into the driveway. Cathryn is outside with Jasmine. "Look! Daddy's home!"

Jasmine squeals in delight. "Dada, Dada," she coos. Cathryn places Jasmine on her dad's lap, and she bounces happily. Stephen kisses her, ruffling her curly brown hair.

"I missed you, my princess," he says, kissing her. Marissa watches the exchange between them as she stands beside Cathryn. She has been home for a few days now and is happy that Stephen is finally home. Oh how she missed him.

Through the days of replaying her last words to Stephen before the accident, Marissa vows to never ever let anything or anyone come between her and Stephen again. She pushes Jason to the back of her mind and decides that is where he will stay.

Stephen rolls into the living room to shouts of "Welcome home, Stephen!" The living room was filled with the smiling faces of family and friends. Sharon walks over and hugs him.

"I'm glad you are home and okay, Stephen," Sharon says to him. Stephen smiles at her and hugs her again.

"I'm glad to be home, Sharon. Glad to be surrounded by friends and family." He reaches for Marissa's hand, and she inches closer to him. He raises her hand to his lips. "Thank you for the days you sat at my bedside singing to me, Sharon. Marissa always told me you had a beautiful voice, and that is an understatement. I thought you were an angel, and I was in heaven when I woke up to your singing. You'll never know how much that meant to me to have you there."

Sharon doesn't miss the shocked expression on her daughter's face as she hugs Stephen.

"I'm just glad you are home, Stevie." Sharon says, hugging him tightly.

Marissa looks over at Jade who is nervously wringing her fingers, grinning, almost close to tears. Never ever has Sharon referred to Stephen as Stevie.

Marissa wonders wryly who this person is impersonating her mom because this Sharon she does not recognize.

The doorbell rings and Nathan walks over to answer. "Is Marissa Paisley home?" the young man at the door asks.

"Yes, can I help you?" Nathan asks suspiciously.

Marissa walks over. "I am Marissa Paisley."
The young man hands her an envelope.

"You've been served," he says and walks away.

CHAPTER 10

Marissa stands in the doorway and watches as the young man walks back down the driveway, gets into his car, and drives off. Marissa knows what is in her hand, but she can't bring herself to acknowledge it.

Natalia walks over to her, "Issa, I have something in my car I need to show you. Can you come take a look?" Marissa looks at her friend questioningly.

Jade walks over. "Oh yes, I remember. Come on, Issa." Marissa follows her sister and friend to Natalia's car.

Natalia takes the envelope from her hand. "I didn't want you to open the envelope in front of all the prying eyes."

"Oh," Marissa says, her brain finally catching up. Marissa is at her breaking point, not sure how much more she can take. She feels like the universe is conspiring against her.

"I think that head injury is kinda still affecting you." Jade says. "You stood there like a deer in headlights, and your brain literally did not turn on for a while."

Marissa laughs. "That's not funny, Jae. You make the most inappropriate jokes."

"You're laughing though," Jade says. "That's all that matters." She hugs her sister.

Natalia reads the contents of the envelope. "It's Jason. He is suing for joint custody of Jasmine." Marissa's knees buckle, and Jade braces her against the car.

"Don't faint on us, Issa. God knows you can't handle another head injury." Jade says, "Breathe. Natalia is way ahead of you on this."

"What do you mean?" Marissa asks

"From the day at the mall, the day Jasmine was born. When I realized who Jason was, I started running background checks on him. I know everything about him down to his credit score," Natalia says. "I figured he would surface at some point. When Stephen called me from the hotel, I knew this would happen, so I started building our case. It will be fine. We will meet with his attorney in two weeks, and we will figure it out. You're not going to lose Jas, so don't even think that."

Marissa holds her now throbbing head, "This is a mess. I made a mess of my life."

"Issa, you didn't. You know Natalia is a badass, so let her do what she does, and you concentrate on getting better and taking care of your family. Okay?" Jade asks. Marissa nods. "And the next time you decide to go out of the country to go find a sperm donor, take us with you. Natalia and I are way better at this than you." Jade and Natalia are laughing, but Marissa is not amused.

"Come on, Issa," says Natalia, "you got to see how funny this is. Of all the men in the world you went and unknowingly picked up a famous country singer all the way over yonder, who just happens to be the same private that your husband saved eons ago, have his baby, left him without a name, then two years later, went on vacation all the way over on another side of yonder with your husband where you then ran into said famous country singer, who now realizes you have his baby, and now wants to share custody."

Marissa glares at a laughing Jade and Natalia.

"She's right, Issa," says Jade, almost to tears with laughter, "It's like your stars are meant to collide. Thank God Stephen knew what you were doing before because you suck at cheating." That makes Natalia and Jade laugh even harder. Marissa could no longer contain herself and she starts to laugh at the mess of it all.

"It's good to see you laughing like this, Sissy." Jade hugs her sister. "I don't know what I would do if I lost you."

The three ladies hug each other, half laughing, half crying. "Let's get back in before Sharon comes out here and accuses me of spoiling her party. We have been BFFs of late, and you just got back in her good graces, so let's not rock the boat," Jade says, laughing at her sister. Marissa scowls at her. "Girl, you know it's the truth. Admit it," she says to Marissa.

Marissa laughs. "I really like this new Sharon though. I finally feel like I have my mother back."

The house is finally empty, and Marissa settles into Stephen's arms. He kisses her hair and rubs her shoulder. "You're tense, Issa. I need you to relax, babe. Natalia is an excellent attorney; she knows what she is doing." Marissa kisses Stephen. "Tomorrow is another day. Tonight, we sleep, tomorrow we fight. Okay?" Stephen says.

The surety in Stephen's voice relaxes her. "Okay." she says in agreement. Marissa gives in to the tiredness washing over her and drifts off to sleep. Stephen lays still, holding her close. He does not want to let go. Tears stream down his face at the thought of leaving Marissa and Jasmine in uncertainty. Life has robbed him of his limbs, his manhood, and now his family.

Stephen is not a praying man, but in that moment, he finds himself praying. He secretly thanks Sharon for the prayers she prayed at his bedside while he was in the hospital.

"Father, I know I haven't spoken to you in... well, maybe never. My mom and Sharon are sure that you are there and that you exist. So I am asking you to protect my family when I am gone. I am praying that you will show Issa her strength; sometimes she doesn't see it. I pray that you will surround my daughter with wonderful friends and one day a wonderful husband. I pray that Issa will find love without guilt, and I pray that Saunders will drop this lawsuit...ummm...thank you...I'm done...ummm, Amen." Stephen looks around the room as if waiting for a response. When nothing happens, he snuggles closer to Marissa and drifts off to sleep.

***

Birds sing the sky awake as Marissa yawns and stretches. She hears Jasmine over the baby monitor giggling as Stephen sings to her. They are one week out from the custody case, the thought of which still has Marissa rather uneasy.

Marissa walks down the hall to Jasmine's room. She watches Stephen as he changes Jasmine, still singing softly to her. "Now let's go see if Mommy is awake," Stephen says, kissing his daughter. He turns and sees Marissa standing there. "Well, what do you know? Mommy is awake." Stephen tickles a giggling Jasmine.

Marissa smiles at them, kisses Stephen then Jasmine's freckled cheeks. "How's your day today, Issa? Stephen asks.

"I'm clear for the most part of the day," Marissa says, looking at him curiously.

"I need to spend some time with you. Can we drop off Jas to Sharon?"

"I'm sure it won't be a problem." Marissa smiles at Stephen, intrigued. "I'll call her. What do you have in mind?"

Stephen smiles at her, "There's a basket on the table downstairs. Remind me to grab that when we are leaving."

"Okay, I'll go call Mom." Marissa says excitedly. Stephen watches as she disappears with Jasmine down the hall. He takes out his phone and dials.

"Hello, Saunders?"

On the other end of the line Jason answers. "Yes."

"We need to talk."

"Who is this? Colonel Paisley?"

"Yes."

"With all due respect, sir, I think it is best if you talk with my attorney."

"Listen, we need to talk. I know you are in town. I know you bought a house here. Meet me at the VA cafe on March Street today...say around five?" There's dead silence on the other end. "Listen, I hate to do this, but you owe me, so be there."

Jason hesitates for a moment, "That's low, Colonel, but I will meet you there."

***

Evidence of spring fills the park as Marissa and Stephen lay on the grass looking up at the clear blue sky. Stephen reaches for her hand and brings it to his lips. "It's so peaceful out today," Marissa says. Stephen pulls her head closer and kisses the back of her head.

"Issa, my darling, you know I love you and Jas with my whole heart, right?"

Marissa laughs jokingly. "With my whole heart, I know this." She stops smiling when she realizes that Stephen is being serious. She sits up, looking down at him. Worry covers her face. Stephen's face says something is seriously wrong. She isn't sure if she can handle anything else.

As if sensing her thought, Stephen says, "Issa, I want you to know that you are so much stronger than you think. You are an amazing wife and mother, and it has been my privilege loving you."

"Babe, your eyes and your voice say something is wrong, and I need you to tell me," Marissa says, her voice full of worry.

Stephen kisses her hands again, his eyes never leaving hers. He knows what he is about to say will pain her deeply. He already wishes that he could undo what has not yet been said. He searches but cannot find a gentle way to break the news to her. "Issa, during surgery the doctors found a tumor in my brain."

Marissa gasps, but Stephen continues. He might as well get it out. "It's cancer, glioblastoma. It's inoperable and there's no cure. The doctors gave me five to six months to live."

Marissa lets out a soul-piercing wail. Stephen knows that to the very day he dies he will never forget that sound. Marissa collapses on him, crying. Stephen hugs her and they weep together.

"There must be something we can do, babe. We can fight this. We won't give up," Marissa says through her tears.

"No, babe. I have some of the best doctors in the army checking, and so far, nothing." He kisses her lips. "I just want to spend the rest of my days loving you and Jas. You made me the happiest man in the world that day when you agreed to give me your number. After much pleading, of course." They chuckled. "I am still the happiest man in the world today, Issa, and I will remain that way until I leave this earth. You are my whole heart, and I will love you forever and the day after that and the day after that." Marissa hugs Stephen and cries even harder.

"I've made some good investments, so you and Jasmine will be well taken care of." Stephen continues. "Plus, luckily, I increased my insurance policy before all of this, so you guys will be good. You don't have to work if you don't want to."

"All the money in the world is not you, Stephen. What I want is our life together, all our firsts with Jasmine. This is not fair, Stephen. This can't be happening." Marissa breaks down again; this time she is inconsolable.

"I know. I would give anything to have a hundred years with you," he says, kissing her. "But you will be okay, Marissa. You and Jasmine will be fine." Marissa kisses him deeply.

"I won't be because you won't be with me," she sobs.

"I'll always be with you." Stephen folds Marissa in his arms as they cry.

***

Marissa is lost in thought as they drive to her parent's house. A life without Stephen makes no sense, and a world where Stephen is not a part of does not exist. "Issa, can you drop me at the VA Cafe on March Street? I'll take a cab home. I have to meet an old army friend."

Marissa looks at him curiously but does not question him. Anything Stephen needs at this point, in her book, she would move heaven and earth to get it to him. He reaches for her hand and kisses it. "It will be fine, I promise."

"It can't be fine, Stephen. You're dying. How can that be fine?" Marissa says, blinking back tears. She pulls over to gather herself. Stephen hugs her as she cries.

She composes herself and pulls back onto the road. Soon she pulls into the parking lot of the VA Cafe.

She deftly pulls out Stephen's wheelchair, fighting back tears. She attempts to wheel Stephen in.

"Issa, let me do this. I'll meet you at home."
He kisses away the worried look on her face. "It will be okay. I promise."

"So you keep saying, babe, but it's not." Marissa's voice breaks again, and the tears start streaming.

"I hate to leave you like this, but I really need to meet with my buddy," Stephen says. "Will you be okay driving?"

Marissa kisses him deeply, "Go have fun with your buddy. I promise I'll be okay."

"Now who is lying?" Stephen says, kissing her again. "I'll be home soon, I promise." Stephen watches as Marissa gets in the car and drives away. His heart hurts, but he knows he will not rest well if he doesn't face Jason.

***

Jasmine is bouncing on Graham's lap as Marissa enters. She has to muster all her strength not to burst into tears again at the sight of Jasmine. How will she explain it when Stephen is gone?

Graham sees the look on Marissa's face, and she knows that he already knows.

"Sharon is in the kitchen, Peanut," he says, kissing her. "I need some more Princess Jasmine time. We are about to serve tea," he says, laughing. Marissa kisses Jasmine and ruffles her hair.

As she walks in the kitchen, Sharon and Jade are at the table. Both of them rush to hug her as she bursts into tears.

Marissa wonders if her tear ducts will ever run empty because she sure has cried so much in recent days.

"How did you guys know?" Marissa asked through her tears.

"Cathryn and Nathan told us at the hospital, but Stephen asked that he be the one to tell you. I'm sorry to have kept it from you, my princess, but I couldn't take that from him. I have caused him, you, both of you so much hurt, and I am truly sorry." Marissa hugs her mom and sister, and they cry even harder.

"I think God is punishing me, Mom. All these years, you were right. There are consequences to our actions, and now Stephen is dying, and I may lose my daughter. But I still can't help but ask, how can something so beautiful come from wrong?" she wails.

"Marissa, darling, God doesn't work like that. He's not out there trying to get you. God offers grace through his son Jesus. It's that same grace that forgives me for the many ways I have wronged you as a mother and as a Christian. It's that same grace that forgives you for anything that you may have done wrong, and that same grace will take Stephen to heaven when the time comes." Sharon hugs her daughter. "I am sorry for the confusion and any way I have misled you both or misrepresented who God is to you. Graham helped me to realize that."

"Dad?" Jade and Marissa ask through their tears.

"Yes, Dad." Sharon laughs, "Turns out he was listening way more than I was in church. He's practically a deacon by my church's standards, but don't tell him I said that. It might just go to his head."

"Dad may take over that pulpit come Sunday," Jade jokes. "Do they have any young deacons there, say my age or a little bit older? I may just show up to church come Sunday." Jade laughs. Sharon and Marissa laugh at the silliness of Jade.

Sharon sits with her two girls at the table. She looks at them. "I love you both so much. I'm blessed to be your mother."

"We love you too, Mommy," they both chime in. They sit at the table holding each other's hands while Sharon prays a prayer of peace, protection, and healing.

Marissa loves this version of her mother, and she's grateful that they have made amends and even more grateful that Jasmine has her Grandma Sharon and Grandnan Cathy.

***

Inside the VA Cafe, Stephen and Jason sip on beers. They stare at nothing in particular behind the bar. "How long do you have?" Jason asks.

"Less than six months," Stephen responds.

"Does Marissa know that you're here?" Jason asks.

"She would kill me if she knew." Stephen and Jason laugh. "She is stubborn like that," Stephen says wryly. "Listen, I saw you two at the hotel. I saw the way you hugged her; I saw you kissed her. I saw how she was with you…"

Jason cuts Stephen off. "I really didn't know she was married, even worse, married to you. I would never break that code, man. You saved my life, and I thank you for that. I would never disrespect you like that. It's just that I saw her. . . I was captivated with her from the moment I saw her, and I have thought of her every single day since we first met. I even wrote a song about her..." Jason's voice trails off.

Stephen rests his hand on Jason's shoulders. "Whisper in the Night," Stephen says.

"How did you know?" Jason asked, putting his face in his palm.

"That night I met you at the hotel, I listened to a bunch of your songs. When I heard that one, I knew you were singing about Issa. She's been intoxicating like that from the very moment I met her. I'm not a songwriter like you," Stephen laughs, "but you penned exactly how I felt about her from the first time I saw her."

Jason laughs a bit uncomfortably. "Laughs aside though, I know you're an honorable man from our time in the army… a hotshot, but an honorable hotshot." Stephen and Jason laugh.

"And I know you didn't break the code," Stephen air quotes code. "Though this may sound weird to you, I can tell that you have feelings for her. I can see that you're in love with her. And even though it pains me to admit it—and I know she will never admit this to me until the day I die—but I think she's in love with you too. It was evident when she returned home and even more evident the night we all met."

Jason shifts uneasily as Stephen continues. "I knew whoever she met that night had taken a place in her heart that only I had held until that time. I was jealous of that person who replaced me. I was even more jealous when I realized it was you. I felt that fate was mean and cruel. The man whose life I saved is now the man my wife is in love with and the man who fathered my daughter."

Stephen turns to look at Jason. "I know I disrespected you and my wife that night, and I am sorry."

Jason looks away from Stephen then down at his boots. "I am in love with her," he admits. His voice was a mere whisper. "I'm sorry, man, but I have been in love with her from the very moment I opened my car door." He looks at Stephen. "Now what do we do?"

"This is what I need you to do. Drop the lawsuit, and you and Marissa work out Jas's well-being outside of the courts." Stephen looks at him. "I can't promise you that Marissa will be with you when I'm gone even though I know she's in love with you. She's a stubborn woman, but I know that if you give her the chance to get to know you, she'll allow you in Jas's life. She's been hurt too much in this life, Saunders, from her dad dying when she was two, to Iraq, to this very day when she learned I have cancer. I can't let that hurt continue. Do you get me, Saunders?"

Stephen looks at Jason. He has a pained look on his face. "Now I know you love her, and I am saying you have my blessing to love her, to love Jas, just don't hurt them. Otherwise, I will kick your ass all the way from heaven." Stephen laughs at Jason as he extends his hand. "Do we have a deal brother?"

Jason takes Stephen's hand. "Yes, I'll drop the case." He looks directly at Stephen as he shakes his hand. "And I will love her and Jasmine whether she will have me or not, and I'll protect them to my dying breath, on my honor," he says. He stands and salutes Stephen, and Stephen salutes him.

Stephen hands Jason an envelope, "Give this to Marissa after I'm gone. You will know when the time is right." Stephen wheels off from Jason but stops abruptly. "And, Saunders, be patient with her, and she will love you like you've never been loved but push her and that door will be closed to you forever."

Jason nods to Stephen awkwardly. He watches as he wheels away. A million thoughts race through his head, but the one he settles on is Marissa. He wonders how she will handle Stephen passing. He wishes that he could run to her, hold her, comfort her, kiss her until it's all better.

But I know what Stephen says is true. For now, will just love you from the shadows, Marissa.

CHAPTER 11

It has been five months since Stephen told Marissa the dreadful news of his diagnosis. His health has declined rapidly, and he has become a shadow of himself.

The days have been filled with Stephen talking about everything and anything to Marissa. He is very intentional about the conversations he has with her in the little time he knows he has left.

Stephen wishes he could spend eternity loving Marissa, and he grimaces at the thought of anyone else but him loving her, but in his heart he knows it's not fair for Marissa to be alone.

He thinks about Jasmine, and he feels the tears sneaking in as he thinks about the fact that he won't be the one to walk her down the aisle. There are so many firsts that he will miss, and it breaks his heart to think about them.

As Marissa sits and looks on the frail frame of her husband, she recognizes the importance of time. She realizes that Stephen's time is limited, and she is intent on maximizing all the time that she can have with him.

Outside of Jasmine, everything stops in her world. Her only focus is Stephen and Jasmine. She is intentional about the things she does and the places she goes. Truth be told, she is scared that if she leaves, Stephen will transition alone.

Sickness and death have a way to bring clarity to one's life, and Marissa is now staring clarity directly in the face. Time suddenly seems like life's most precious commodity.

She realizes that all the time she spent arguing or worrying about the life she did not have when Stephen got injured was all a waste because she now sees that she has so much more.

Her focus on one aspect of their relationship that was no longer has caused her to miss out on everything else that she loved and adored about Stephen and what made her relationship with him amazing.

In this moment Marissa wishes she had a do-over. She would have done so many things differently. She hates that it took Stephen's impending death for her to realize that everything she needed was already wrapped up in her relationship, and all she had to do was slow down and look at what and who God had blessed her with. This thought brought immense sadness to Marissa's heart.

Stephen studies her closely, "What's going on in that pretty little head of yours, Issa?" he manages weakly. "You're miles away."

"I'm right here with you, my love." Marissa says, leaning in to kiss him.

"What are you thinking about?"

Marissa hesitates for a minute, sadness in her eyes. She realizes that she fell trap to envy. She wanted to dance like everyone else. She wanted the wild passionate lovemaking they used to share. She wanted everyone else's love story except the one she had.

Sharon used to say that envy is the curse of mankind. It's the sin that caused the fall in the garden, and Marissa realizes that she fell victim to envy. She spent less time on enjoyment and more time on envy.

Oh, how she wishes she had taken more vacations with him, laughed more, loved more, been in his presence more. Just enjoyed him. Now that he is dying, she wants to simply enjoy the man that he is and enjoy the timeless love that they share.

You can't lie to a dying man," he chuckles.

She looks at him, still sad, "I'm thinking about you, us…just how much time I wasted worrying about…worrying about nothing really," she continues.

"Come here my love," he says reaching for her hand. Marissa obliges and sits beside him on the bed. He kisses her palm gently, "Issa, when I came back from Iraq, I wished I hadn't." He kisses her palm again as he watches the horrified look on her face, but he continues. "I didn't want to burden you. I love you too much for that."

"Babe, no, honey, you were never a burden, babe. I am sorry if I made you feel that way." Marissa kisses his lips.

"You didn't, my love," Stephen continues, "I was ungrateful and bitter. I lashed out at you so many times. I did not want to feel obligated, and I spent more time focused on what I lost without considering what you, what we lost. That was selfish of me, honey, and I am sorry." He kisses her hands once more.

This was now Stephen's moment of clarity, and it was a bitter pill to swallow, but he knows he must. "I am sorry…," his breath is raspy, "I am sorry for not loving you the way I should've. I am sorry for not receiving your love the way I should have. I am sorry for disrespecting you with Saunders." Marissa kisses him and gives him a sip of water.

"You need to rest my love."

"I have eternity to do that," he chuckles.

It amazes Marissa that even at this stage, Stephen is still charming, witty and funny; she couldn't help but laugh with him.

After a bit, her tone grows serious, "I should be the one that is saying sorry, babe. Now don't interrupt me because I have to get this out. No silly jokes, okay?" she says laughing.

"This sounds like it's about to be one of Sharon's sermons," Stephen says half laughing, half coughing, "I may hit eternity before you finish." He laughs as hard as he possible can.

Marissa knows that she will miss Stephen's wit and humor. It is one of the many great things she loves about him. "Babe…" She laughs, "I'm trying to be serious, let me get this out."

"Okay, I'm listening," Stephen says kissing her hand, still laughing.

Marissa smiles at him warningly as she begins, "I want to apologize for any time I've loved you less, looked at you as less than, spoken to you as less than who you are to me, my husband, my king. I want you to know how much I love you. How grateful I am for our love and how blessed I am to be loved by you."

Stephen tries to interrupt but she cuts him off. "For every time I used my words to hurt you, forgive me. For every time I've been upset with you or blamed you for anything, forgive me. For the things I said in the car before the accident, forgive me. Know that I love you. I have loved you from the first time you tried to get my number with your corny line." Marissa laughs even though tears streams down her face.

Stephen laughs and gently wipes them away. "I will never stop loving you," she says "and I want to thank you for our daughter, for the way you love her, the way you love us with your whole heart. You are like no other. Thank you for setting your love on me." She kisses him deeply. "Okay, no more mushy stuff. You need to rest."

Marissa gets up and adjusts the oxygen in Stephen's nose. "You are the most beautiful nurse," Stephen says teasingly, smiling up at Marissa. She fluffs the pillow behind his head and tucks the blanket under his thin frail body.

"Is that comfortable for you, my love?" She asks, gently kissing his lips. She looks at him. Even in sickness, he's still handsome. His stubborn jawline has not faded. Another one of the many things that Marissa loves about him. She has not left his side for a minute, and she refuses to have a nurse take care of him, except to administer medication.

"I'm very comfortable, Issa," Stephen says, his voice a bit hoarse. "Come lay beside me for a bit," he says, weakly taking her hand and trying to pull her to come lay beside him. Marissa snuggles up to his skinny frame. He has lost a lot of weight and barely eats anymore.

Tears sting the back of Marissa's eyes once more, but this time she quickly blinks them back. She will be strong for Stephen and will shed no more tears in his presence.

Stephen takes Marissa's hand and brings it to his lips and kisses it gently. "Issa, you know you are my whole heart, right?" Stephen asks, kissing her hand again.

"And Jas too" Marissa says, half smiling as her voice catches in her throat.

"Yes," Stephen laughs weakly, "And Jas too." He brings Marissa's hand to his heart. "I want to make sure that there is nothing unresolved between us…" Stephen takes a breath and Marissa cuts him off.

"Babe, after 'the sermon,' there is nothing unresolved…" Marissa laughs as she air quotes. Stephen gently squeezes her hand, and Marissa realizes that he is being serious.

"Issa, I've loved you from the first moment I saw you, and I will love you to my last breath, and if possible and God allows it, I will love you even after."

Marissa kisses Stephen. This time the tears start to roll down her face. "I'm not ready to say goodbye, my love. I'm not ready to say goodbye." She cries.

Between many teary kisses Marissa again tells Stephen of her love for him as she pulls him into her arms.

Marissa beckons to Cathryn and Sharon, now standing at the entrance of their bedroom door and they walk in followed by a clearly crying Jade.

Nathan, Jasmine, and Graham follow closely behind. Nathan places Jasmine on the bed beside her mom and dad. Stephen reaches for his daughter and kisses her stubby fingers.

Marissa wonders if Jasmine knows that her dad is dying. Somehow it seems as if she does because she isn't bouncing around as she usually would. Instead she lies beside her dad as he gently strokes her hair.

Cathryn walks over and kisses her son's forehead. Likewise Nathan. Jade is inconsolable and clings helplessly to Graham; he gently strokes her back as she sobs.

Sharon starts to sing *His Eye Is On The Sparrow*. There is a serene stillness in the room as Sharon's soothing golden voice washes over the room, peacefully singing Stephen home as he breathes his last.

***

The bagpipe plays a haunting melody. Marissa
erks as each round of gunfire goes off. Tears stream
own her face. She watches as white doves are
ncaged and take to the skies.

She hears the soulful sound of Sharon singing
Amazing Grace. Beside her, Jade and Natalia wipe
way their tears. Graham holds Jasmine close to him.

She watches as Nathan and Cathryn lay roses on
op of Stephen's casket. The methodical folding of the
American flag by the men in uniform tugs at her heart.

She feared this moment when Stephen was
nlisted. She was grateful the day he was out of the
army even though he was not the same. She was still
hankful for any part of Stephen that she shared.

He was her first, and she has loved him from the
very first moment they met to a few days ago when he
ook his last breath with his head nestled against her
osom.

She has never viewed death as a beautiful thing
before, but her last days with Stephen were beautiful to
his last breath.

Scenes of Stephen looking dashing in his
uniform as he pleaded with her for her phone number
flood her memory.

She reaches over and holds Natalia's
hand. Stephen was her great love, but he was also
Natalia's. Even though Marissa will never break
Stephen's confidence, she knows that Stephen was the
man Natalia would never mention.

She squeezes her friend's hand as Jackson,
Natalia's boyfriend, consoles her weeping friend.

Marissa senses the shadow among the graves. She looks and sees Jason standing a little distance away. He isn't in his regular jeans, T-shirt, and rugged boots. He is fully dressed in his uniform. He stands at attention as the other soldiers bellow out commands.

Marissa kisses the rose in her hand and lays it on Stephen's simple wooden casket. She watches as dirt falls on the pine box. This was goodbye and she's not sure if she can survive doing life without Stephen, yet she knows she must carry on, not just for herself, but most importantly for Jasmine. "Until we meet again, my love." She whispers, "I love you with my whole heart. Forever and the day after."

Marissa looks up and Jason is no longer there. She is sure that he was there though. It warms her heart that he showed up to pay his respects to the man who sacrificed much for him. Stephen had finally shared in detail with Marissa the dreadful incident that took so much from them both.

Marissa watches as the funeral goers thin out. She isn't ready to leave just yet. She needs to see them lower Stephen. Maybe that will bring some acceptance that he is no longer with her. Tears stream down her face as they lower him into the ground.

Marissa feels a hand around her shoulder. She knows it is her mother before she even turns to look. Sharon's arms are waiting as her daughter cries uncontrollably.

Sharon too was here once before, watching as they lowered Colton, and Marissa was Jasmine, not understanding much of what was happening. She hugs her daughter tightly, knowing she has a long road ahead of her with many tearful nights.

Her heart breaks in a million pieces for her daughter, yet she has hope. She prays that Marissa will find love and happiness again, the way she has with Graham.

In the distance, Jason watches as Sharon comforts Marissa. He wishes that he could run to her and take her in his arms and hold her close until her crying subsides, but he knows he must keep his distance, at least for now.

One thing he is sure of, when the time is right, he will be there for Jasmine and Marissa if they will have him. Until then, Jason is content with simply waiting.

***

It's been a year since Stephen's death, and the days have been long and the nights even longer, lonely and empty. Through many long unending, pointless days, and agonizingly tearful nights, Marissa has somehow made it through.

She is grateful for the help of her and Stephen's families. She wouldn't have made it without them.

She is finally at the place where she is ready to donate Stephen's things and sell their house. Natalia and Jade are at Marissa's house helping her pack away Stephen's things.

Natalia stares at a picture of Stephen, her, and Marissa. It was their early college years. Even then things were complicated. They had slept together a few months earlier, but Natalia told Stephen that she couldn't handle a relationship with a soldier even though she knew in her heart of hearts that she loved him.

Her greatest fear was hearing a knock on the door and the army reporting that Stephen had died. She knew she couldn't handle it, so she broke it off.

She looks over at her friend. She has been a tower of strength for Stephen. Marissa did not leave Stephen's bedside for a moment when he was hurt. Natalia found new respect for her friend in those moments.

Over the years she watched Marissa in amazement as she remained faithful to Stephen, loving him through all the challenges even when she knew that a vital part of their relationship was taken from them. Likewise, in the last months of Stephen's life, Marissa was the same attentive, loving wife, pouring her everything into ensuring Stephen's last days were surrounded by love.

Natalia wipes the tears that suddenly well up in her eyes. She has kept her love for Stephen hidden all these years, but she hears herself blurt out. "Stephen and I slept together when we were in college, but I swear it was before he met you, and it was only once." Natalia covers her face, afraid to look at Marissa. Marissa turns and looks at her friend. She smiles at her.

"Well, that was very unexpected." She laughs.

"Issa, did you hear what I said?" Natalia asks.

"I heard you." Marissa said, looking intently at her friend.

"Please don't hate me." Natalia begs, "Stephen wanted to tell you from the moment he realized we were friends, but I asked him not to. I was afraid it would hurt our friendship."

The silence hangs in the air, as Marissa stares at her friend.

"Issa, say something, please. Anything. Please, please, please don't hate me."

Marissa laughs at Natalia. "Girl, stop! I was just doing the dramatic pause for effect." Marissa laughs even harder at the petrified look on Natalia's face.

"Are you really joking at this time, Issa?" Natalia says, still confused.

"Yes, I know that Stephen is…was the nameless, faceless love of your life, the one whose name you would never mention," Marissa admits.

Natalia turns away from her friend and walks toward the window.

Marissa strolls over to her friend and places her hand on her shoulder and turns her to face her. "Nat, I could never hate you, and I wasn't mad at you when Stephen told me a few months before he died."

She looks directly at her friend. "What I was though was sad. Sad that you didn't trust our friendship enough to tell me, and it hurt me that you had to carry that secret around for so long... but no, I could never hate you. I know you and Stephen were trying to protect me."

Marissa hugs Natalia. "Now it's my time to protect you. You can cry, scream, grieve. Whatever you choose. I know that you loved him, Nat, and he loved you, and you need to grieve him the way you helped me grieve."

"I loved him, Issa, but you were his forever love. I saw that the moment he walked into El Cilantro Tacos. He was smitten. My best friend had the love of the man that I loved. His heart was taken from that moment, and I knew he would never look at me or any other woman the way he looked at you. I was happy and content to let whatever love I felt go because I knew you both loved each other. If there was ever a meant-to-be story, it was you and Stephen." Natalia hugs her friend. "I'm sorry I kept it from you, and I am grateful you're not mad at me."

"You're my girl, my sister, Nat. Nothing changes that. I love you. You know that, right?"

"I know," Natalia says, "and I love you." She hugs her friend tightly. She is relieved that this secret no longer looms between them.

The doorbell rings, interrupting their sisterly moment.

Jade bellows from below. "Issa!" Jade yells. Marissa runs down the stairs.

Standing in her doorway, looking amazingly handsome in his usual rugged jeans, T-shirt, and boots, is Jason. She drinks him in. She hasn't seen him since the funeral, and their last communication was the letter he sent from his attorney to Natalia a few days after Marissa learned of Stephen's illness. The letter advised that he was no longer seeking joint custody of Jasmine.

Jason stares at her. Marissa feels naked under his eyes as he looks at her from head to toe.

"Marissa, hi..." She senses his uncertainty. Jade stares at both of them.

"Jae, Nat, can you give us a few minutes?"

"Okay, but I'm right in the kitchen, not too far from the shotguns!" Jade announces while walking away. Marissa laughs to herself. Jade knows there are no shotguns in the house. Stephen always said he was around enough guns in the army and didn't want any in his house.

"May I come in?" he asks.

Marissa holds the door and Jason steps past her. He smells delicious. Whatever cologne he is wearing had her senses twirling back to a night long ago, one that is ever present in her memory.

Jason looks at Marissa. He wonders if it is possible for her to get more beautiful every time he sees her. The floral sundress that she is wearing shows off her freckled neck and shoulders.

Something about the sunlight streaming through the huge bay windows that dances playfully through her hair makes her look tantalizing and irresistible. It takes all his strength not to pull her close to him and kiss her passionately until her lips are bruised and she is longing for him.

"How have you been?" Marissa tries to make small talk. Jason is still caught up in the sight of her. "Jason?"

He snaps back to the present. "Umm…good." He's still flustered and fidgets awkwardly with an envelope in his hand. "How are you and Jasmine? I mean…" He stutters, "Umm…How are you coping?" *She must think I'm a babbling idiot.*

"We're good…" Marissa, says a bit hesitantly. Jason doesn't miss the change in her tone. "Jas is not here…Ummm."

Jason hates that he placed her in that situation with requesting shared custody. If there was an undo button, he would have taken it. He can sense that Marissa doesn't trust him, and he knows he needs to fix that.

"Stephen asked me to give you this." He handed the envelope to her.

She looks at him, confused. Jason continues trying to reassure her silently that he is not there to cause trouble., "He met me at the VA Cafe a few months before he passed."

Marissa remembers that day. "I dropped him there that day. He said he was meeting an old friend," Marissa says suspiciously.

"I'm the old friend," he says, smiling. "We spoke for a while."

"That's why you dropped the custody case," Marissa muses out loud.

"He didn't want to cause you any more hurt, and he made me see that if I had continued, that was what I would be doing. And I lo...care about you too much to want to hurt you in any way."

Marissa stares at Jason and smiles. Jason is relieved; he realizes that he has missed seeing her smile. All he wants to do is hold her in his arms and kiss her and have her look at him the way she did that night. Instead, he treads lightly, not wanting to scare her away. "I am gonna go so you can read the letter, but I'd like to call you sometime to make arrangements to see Jasmine, completely on your terms though," he says, holding up his hand reassuringly to Marissa. "No pressure. Whenever you're ready, I'll be here."

"I'd like that too," Marissa hears herself say.

"Ummm..I'm performing at the stadium in town and I want you to come… I mean I would like it if you came… and also will you have dinner with me?" Jason asked, rambling on. "…I mean, after my concert we could have dinner, or you could just come to the concert… but I'd like to take you to dinner, but if you are not ready, I also understand." Jason feels like a babbling teenager asking the most popular girl in school to the prom.

Marissa laughs at his nervousness, "You're asking for a lot, but yes, I would like to go to the concert, and I would like to have dinner too." Jason hugs her tightly then quickly lets her go. His arms were familiar, and Marissa felt safe there. She secretly wishes that he had held her just a moment longer. She admits to herself that she is longing for his touch.

He avoids her eyes, "Okay, I'll call you to arrange it."

"I'll be waiting." Marissa says teasingly. She watches as Jason jumps in his truck and drives off.

Behind her Natalia and Jade scream. "I'll be waiting?" they ask.

"Someone has learned to flirt," Jade teased.

Marissa laughs. "I was not flirting. He just wants to see his daughter. That's all."

"Uh-huh, then why are your cheeks so flushed?" Nat asks as her friend covers her cheeks.

"So what's that?" Jade asked.

"It's a letter from Stephen, but I would rather open it when I'm alone." She looks at Jade and Natalia. "You both understand, right?" They both nod, hugging her.

"Call us if you need us. I'm sure Mom will keep Jas for the night to give you some time to be alone." Marissa hugs her sister and friend.

"I am the luckiest girl in the world. I couldn't have gotten through these times without both of you," Marissa says, teary-eyed.

"You are the luckiest girl in the world." Jade added, "After all, you have country superstar Jason Saunders swooning over you."

"He wasn't swooning." Marissa laughs. "He did look delicious though, like extremely delicious," she added. Marissa kisses them and watches them leave.

As soon as she closes the door, she sits down on the sofa and grabs her blanket. With trembling fingers, she opens the letter. As she reads, she can hear Stephen's voice echoing in her head.

"Issa, my love, you're my whole heart. I gave Saunders this letter the day I told you that I was sick. It's the day I accepted in my heart that I was okay with you loving him and him loving you. I want you to know that you have my blessing. I want you to love fiercely. Enjoy every fleeting moment that this life offers and don't spend your days mourning me. There is too much of you to love for you to be alone. Saunders is a good man, and he loves you. I now see that my sacrifice saving his life that day was for him to be around to love my two favorite girls. Love again, Issa. Love with your whole heart. Love the way that I have loved you. You and Jas are my whole heart, and if you close your eyes, you can still feel my love surrounding you. Until we meet in the land that never ends, I am forever yours. Stephen.

P.S. Stop crying, go to my closet, to the back of the closet, and you will see my white uniform. I placed it all the way back there so you wouldn't bury me in that."

Marissa laughs at Stephen's humor.

"Now if you buried me in it, then what I'm about to say will be useless unless you exhume me...fyi please don't." Marissa is laughing so hard at this point.

"Open the box, and what you find inside, those are my last gifts to you and Jas. You will know when to add to them. I love you, my darling. Now go because I know you love a good treasure hunt. Forever yours. Stephen...yeah, I'm aware I said that already."

Marissa hugs the pillow close to her and cries and laughs all at the same time. Stephen was an amazing man. Even in death, he was still making her laugh.

She puts down the letter and races up the stairs, taking them two at a time. Stephen knew her all too well; she does love a good treasure hunt.

As promised, in the back of his closet his white uniform is securely tucked almost out of sight. She has to dig to get to it. In the pocket, she finds a blue velvet jewelry box. She runs her fingers over the smoothness of the box. She hesitates. Smiling, she kisses the box and holds it to her heart.

Now crying, she pulls the box open. Inside are two golden heart-shaped lockets and a note that says, 'To the girls who hold my entire heart."

Marissa cries even more. She opens the first locket, and it has a picture of Jasmine, maybe at about six months old. The other side is blank. The inscription reads, *Whisper in the Night*. Marissa holds it close to her heart. She places it around her neck.

She opens the second locket. Inside is a picture of her. It is a picture Stephen took of her on their first date. The other side of the locket is also blank. The inscription reads *Summer Sun*. Marissa rocks her mind. She wonders why Stephen would have used that term. She tries to place it. Somehow, she knows it but not sure from where.

"Give me a clue, babe, give me a clue." Marissa says out loud as she tries to figure out the term *Whisper in the Night* and *Summer Sun.* She draws a blank.

Stephen was usually the one that was good at the clues; she's always good at finding the treasure. "What a pair we made, babe," Marissa whispers to the empty room. "I really miss you."

Marissa thinks for a moment then races down the stairs and rereads the letter. Suddenly it dawns on her. She opens her phone to Jason's album and clicks on the track *Whisper in the Night.* As she listens, she hears it. *Let's make babies with eyes that look like the summer sun...* She rewinds the track. Jason's voice croons through her phone, *You've my heart, girl, I'm yours. Let's make babies with eyes that look like the summer sun.* Marissa stops the track.

"Oh Stephen," she cries. "I understand now." Tears find their familiar path down Marissa's face. She curls herself in a ball and cries. Stephen has given her and Jasmine the permission to let him go. To move on, to live, to love again. Marissa has no doubt that Stephen's love for her and Jasmine is indeed endless.

***

Marissa walks toward the rear entrance door of the stadium. She isn't sure why she's so nervous. She has watched several clips of Jason performing before, but this is the first time she will be seeing him perform live.

She walks over to the guard standing at the door. A giggling Natalia and Jade are close behind. As Marissa approaches, the guard quickly checks the iPad in his hand. He smiles at her as if he knows her. "Marissa Paisley," she says.

"Ahh yes," says the guard, "we are expecting you." He signals to a leggy blonde lady and her petite frame saunters over. She was gorgeous. Her tight fitted leather suit left nothing to the imagination. "Take them directly to the VIP section."

Jade giggles with excitement. "We have certainly arrived. We are about to see The Jason Saunders live in concert, not from the bleachers, I might add, but from the VIP section!" Jade says gleefully. Marissa and Natalia laugh. "Maybe I will find my Jason tonight," says Jade hopefully.

"First of all, he is not my Jason," Marissa says defensively, "and secondly, I am just here as a friend. Nothing more."

"Right, keep telling yourself that, Sissy, keep telling yourself that," says Jade, laughing. "The blush on your face says differently though." Jade and Natalia laugh, and Marissa is not in the least bit amused.

The leggy blonde leads them to their seats directly in front of center stage. The stadium was already packed, and the active chatter mingled with the band sounds like a newly disturbed beehive.

Marissa looks around, hoping to get a glimpse of Jason. Her stomach is in a million knots, and she feels giddy with a mixture of excitement and nervousness.

She hasn't seen Jason since he showed up at her door with the letter from Stephen. They have spoken on the phone a few times, mainly about the arrangements for tonight's show.

There have been long awkward pauses in the conversation with so much unspoken, yet understood, in the silence. Even over the phone Marissa can feel their connection and it is familiar and fleetingly exciting.

Marissa knows she wants to explore more of those feelings. She hasn't done this in a long time, and she may be way off base, but if her senses are correct, Marissa feels that Jason also wants to explore those feelings as well.

Backstage, Jason paces back and forth. He has performed to countless packed arenas and stadiums, ye somehow, tonight, knowing that Marissa is in the audience, has his stomach doing somersaults.

He has sung to her many times before in his head, the countless nameless faces, a representation of the woman who still haunts his dreams. Tonight, however, is different. She is here in person, and this time, every note he sings, she will be right there to hear them. He has dreamed of this moment many times, and now that it is here, it is like déjà vu.

His heart is beating rapidly in his chest. It is so loud, it almost blocks out the thundering sound of screaming fans. *Pull it together dude. You got this,* he says to himself reassuringly. *It's just a girl. Dude, it's not just a girl.* He contradicts himself. "It's Marissa," he said out loud.

The leggy blonde walks in, "It's showtime!" Jason looks at her questioningly. She smiles at him, "Yes, she's here."

"Good," Jason says, relieved. He does some kind of jog on the spot, cricks his neck side to side, rotates his shoulder, shakes his fingers kind of stuff, and the leggy blonde looks at him with wondrous amusement.

"You're nervous," she laughs, looking at him doing this newly ridiculous routine. "Some girl has the great Jason Saunders nervous." She laughs even harder.

"No, I'm not!" he says in a hushed tone, grinning at her. "Come on, let's get this show on the road." Jason has never said that before. It even sounds weird to him coming out of his mouth. *I've got to pull it together.*

To Marisa, the roar of the crowd is deafening. She struggles to hear her own voice in her head. The energy in the arena is electrifying and mind-boggling. She feels herself being drawn in, and Jason has not yet taken the stage.

She is conscious of her heart pounding in her chest just as Jason emerges. Her breath catches in her throat, and Marissa smiles to herself. *God sure did take his time when he made this one.*

The fans are in a frenzy, and Natalia and Jade are no different. They were like lovestruck teenage fans screaming at the boyband with the hot teen heartthrob.

Jason walks to the center of the stage with an air of confidence around him. He grabs hold of the microphone, his voice sultry and sexy. "Kansas City, how are you doing?" His voice is almost like a whisper, but the crowd goes wild.

Jason smiles wryly and in that oh so sultry tone says, "Kansas City, are you ready?" His voice, now booming, echoes across the arena. The fans go even more wild.

Jason starts crooning over the microphone to the screaming audience. As he sings, his eyes are busy scanning the crowd trying to find that face, the one that has haunted his dreams for many moons, Marissa.

Our eyes met, across the aisle, I looked upon your face.

Your brown skin, your sexy eyes, flashed across my mind.

Hand outstretched, I whispered your name, Déjà in my head.

My mind rewinds visions of you, you baby, love making in the sand...

Déjà, Déjà, Déjà Vu, I know, I've kissed you many times,

Déjà, Déjà, Déjà Vu, I know, I've loved you from another time...

Jason's voice washes over Marissa like liquid honey—smooth, velvety, rich, intoxicating, and inviting—every note caresses her very soul. She isn't sure if she has heard this song before, but the crowd loves every sexy note he sings.

The excitement is evident. Marissa looks over at her sister and best friend; they are having the time of their lives. She laughs to herself. When did they become Jason groupies? They are screaming and just doing the most, hanging on to each note as Jason sings.

With every note and every strum of his guitar, Jason envisions Marissa. From his vantage point it is hard to see in the crowd, but he knows she is there. His heart races at the thought of her watching him sing.

Finally his eyes zero in on her, and he inches a little closer to the front of the stage as he continues to sing. *Déjà, Déjà, Déjà Vu, I know, I've kissed you many times,*

Déjà, Déjà, Déjà Vu, I know, I've loved you from another time...

He smiles broadly at her, and she smiles at him. Natalia and Jade go wild. Jason grins at a frantic Jade and Natalia jumping up and down with excitement.

The sight of Marissa energizes him to sing, and he bellows out song after song, all as an ode to her.

As he wraps up his final song, he knows he wants to see Marissa up close, but he dares not venture into the crowd. "This one is for a very special lady in the audience tonight," he says, sweat dripping down his face and his sweat soaked T-shirt clings to his muscular frame. "Thank you for being here tonight."

Jason is looking directly at Marissa, and she feels like he can see through her very soul even from up on the stage. "This one is for you." His eyes never leave hers. He starts to sing *Whisper in the Night*, and the crowd, along with Jade and Natalia, goes crazy.

Marissa stands there looking up at him, receiving every note that he sings. Each note undresses her, until her heart is bare before him. Marissa realizes that she is helplessly attracted and hopelessly in love with this man. *Ay Dios Mio*. She gazes lovingly up at him. He smiles as if he knowingly read her thoughts.

As Jason closes his set, the security from before finds Marissa and leads her, Jade, and Natalia backstage. "Maybe I will ask Jason to autograph my breast," Jade giggles.

"Jade-Ann Swanson!" Marissa laughs at her sister. "You will do no such thing!"

"But that's what fans do, and I am officially a Jason Saunders fan!" Jade says, laughing at her sister.

"That is so not lady-like." Marissa says laughing at her sister.

"Now you sound like Mom," Jade says, now laughing at the horrified look on her sister's face.

"Be glad I did not jump on stage and grab him and do unspeakable things to him" Natalia says. "He was all sweaty and hot, just on stage there singing and looking like a perfect chocolate snack."

"A milk chocolate snack," Jade chimes in.

"He is kinda hot, isn't he," Marissa says, laughing. "I do love me some good chocolate." She laughs. The smile quickly vanishes from Marissa's face as she turns the corner and sees the very leggy blonde, Jason's arms all wrapped around her as she clings to him. Marissa immediately turns and walks aways.

"Marissa, wait!" Jason says, as he catches up to her in a few steps.

"For what, Jason? Wait for what?" Marissa asks. There is so much going on in Jason's head at this moment, but nothing audible comes from his lips. He can see the anger seething from Marissa's very pores.

"Umm, Umm." Still nothing audible comes out.

"That's what I thought!" Marissa's eyes shoot daggers at him. Tears sting the back of her eyes, and she wills the tears back. There is absolutely no way she is going to let him see her cry. "Goodbye, Jason."

Marissa turns and walks off with Natalia and Jade following behind her mouths wide open, dumbfounded. In that moment, Marissa is grateful that she waited before introducing him to Jasmine.

Jason watches helplessly as Marissa walks off. He still cannot find the words to explain to her what she thought she saw.

What was supposed to be an unforgettable night ended up with Marissa walking away from him yet again, and this time it may be for good. "I could really use a sign from you, Colonel. I really messed this up."

CHAPTER 12

It has been a week since Jason watched Marissa walked away from him after his concert. He has not mustered up the courage to call her.

Jason is sprawled on the couch in his apartment. His hair is unkempt, and a week-old beard covers his face.

The curtains are drawn, and even though it is bright outside, in the apartment it is dark and gloomy. Clothes are tossed around. Empty beer cans add to the sloppy decor along with an opened bag of chips, the remnant of its contents scattered on the center table.

The sound of keys turning in the door bring Jason slightly out of his funk. He looks up to see his sister, Tamar, and his niece, Savannah, the leggy blonde from his concert, entering. Tamar glances around the apartment.

She shakes her head disapprovingly as she sees her brother lying there like his world has just ended.

Her short stocky arms across her chest, she glares at him. "Jason Edward Saunders, this place is a mess! You can't hibernate here forever," says Tamar. This time you actually know who and where she is, so go explain to her that it is a big misunderstanding."

Jason is now in a seated position. "Tammy, you didn't see her face. She was seriously furious with me," Jason replies.

"Of course she was," Savannah chimes in. "Someone is always mistaking me for your girlfriend, so why would she be any different? You should go get her, Uncle Jase. No one wants to watch you moping around here for the unforeseeable future."

"The last time she walked out your life, you canceled several tour dates and disappeared up in some mountain in Utah for weeks. We are not doing that this time," Tamar says matter-of-factly. "You're obviously in love with this girl. Why, I don't know, but you are, so go get her."

Jason looks at Tamar and Savannah as if pondering what to do. "What do I do? What do I say?" he asks them.

They throw several suggestions at him but none of them appeal to him. "Marissa is not your regular kind of girl. Jewelry, flowers, doesn't impress her. She'd probably throw them at my head faster than I could say hello."

"Like, I said," Tamar says, "I am not sure what it is about this girl that has you so discombobulated. There are a million girls out there who would gladly be Mrs. Jason Saunders."

"A million girls aren't Marissa, Tammy. There's only one Marissa. She's unique, one of a kind. There is no duplicate. There is none like her, and when you get to know her, you will see what I mean," Jason says, daring his sister to contradict him.

"You're hopelessly sprung," his sister says. "At least do something about it and stop moping around. I hate to see you like this." She hugs him, "So how are you gonna fix this?"

He hugs his sister tightly and finally, he gets up. "Okay, here's the plan. I'll show up at her doorstep….again."

"And do or say what?" they ask.

"That's as far as I have gotten, but hey, it's a start, right?" He laughs awkwardly.

"Please, please, at least take a shower first," say Savannah and her mom, laughing. "You don't want her to turn you away this time simply because you reek."

Jason sniffs both his armpits. "I smell nothing, but okay, I'll shower. I need everything in my favor right now." He kisses his sister and niece and heads to the shower.

"Do you think Marissa will give him a chance?" Savannah asks her mom.

"Well…," Tamar ponders, "if she is the fireball that Jason says that she is, she will make him sweat a bit, but hopefully she knows what a wonderful man my brother is and how lucky she is to have his love, and that will make her come to her senses." Tamar trails off, deep in thought, "Otherwise I may have to have a few words with Little Miss Perfect One of a Kind, myself," she concludes.

"Mom...," pleads Savannah, "promise me you will stay out of Uncle Jase's business. You know he hates when you meddle." She looks at her mom warningly. "Furthermore, I would like to meet my baby cousin before you chase them off."

Tamar smiles at her daughter. "I said talk, not meddle."

"Your version of talking is meddling. Let Uncle Jase figure this out on his own. Okay, Mom?"

Tamar nods, but under her breath she whispers, "I can't make any promises."

***

Jason walks up the stone pathway to Marissa's door. He hesitates for a bit, takes a deep breath, then finally rings the doorbell.

After what feels like an eternity, Marissa opens the door, Jasmine hanging on to her dress trying to see who is there. Jason looks at her then at Jasmine. They are incredibly beautiful, and he knows he wants to spend his life loving them both. Words elude him and he cannot think of what to say.

Marissa looks at Jason. She is taken aback seeing him at her door, as her eyes longingly drink him in. He looks heart-skipping perfect, from his loose-fitting T-shirt, black jeans, and rugged boots to his freshly shaven face, and muscular arms, topped off with his delicious smell. Marissa stares on, at a loss for words.

Finally after the long awkward stares between Marissa and Jason, Jasmine babbles, "Pizza!" which brings them both back to the present.

"Um…Oh…no…not pizza yet, Jas. Soon enough," says Marissa, scooping her up. "Do you want to go finish coloring? Mommy will be right there to help you finish. Is that okay?" she says, kissing Jasmine's cheeks. Jasmine giggles, gives her mom a sloppy wet kiss, wiggles her way out of her mom's arms, and disappears inside the house.

Jason looks at the money in Marissa's hand. "I guess she thought I was the pizza guy, huh?"

"Yes, she's a ham and pineapple pizza kind of girl. She never gets tired of it," Marissa responds, smiling.

"I am a ham and pineapple pizza kind of guy too. Like father like dau…" Jason's words trail off.

There is another long awkward pause as Jason tries to search for the right words to say. Finally, he speaks, "Marissa, I am really sorry about what you think you saw at the concert…"

Marissa interrupts, "You don't owe me any explanation, Jason. What's done is done. I believe we already said our goodbyes the other night, so there's nothing else to say." Her hand was on the door preparing to close it.

"Colonel said you were stubborn, but man, you're seriously stubborn. Give me a chance to explain, then you can close the door." Jason is desperate. He can see the stubbornness in her stance, and he knows he has to choose his words carefully. "Just give me one minute," he pleads. Marissa nods her head in a defiant manner.

As a last act of desperation, he reaches for his phone and video calls Savannah. She picks up on the first ring.

"Hi, Uncle Jase, don't tell me you chickened out already," Savannah blurts out.

Jason turns the screen to Marissa. She recognizes the beautiful blonde from the concert. Anger then a bit of embarrassment but mostly confusion sets in. Jason sees his chance and he takes it. "Marissa, this is my niece, Savannah." Marissa stares dumbfounded at the screen.

"And this is his baby sister, Tamar," Tamar chimes in, her face filling the screen. "Wow, you are a gorgeous one. I can see why my brother is head over heels for you."

"Mom!" says Savannah, "You have no filter!" Tamar laughs, shushing her daughter.

"Marissa, I can't wait to meet you. I can't wait to meet my niece. Did Jason tell you that Jasmine was our mother's name?" Tamar rattles on.

Jason realizes that this is not one of his best ideas. "Ladies, I have to go. I will call you later." He hangs up the phone as Tamar protests.

He turns to Marissa. "I'm sorry. That was dumb. I kinda placed you on the spot there. I was desperate. I mean I am truly sorry. That was not my best or brightest idea."

Just then the pizza delivery guy walks up the driveway. Jason watches as Marissa deftly pays him, smiles sweetly, and collects the pizza. She has yet to acknowledge Jason's apology. Jason patiently waits for the pizza delivery guy to leave before he continues. "I'm sorry. That was not the plan."

"What exactly was the plan, Jason?" Marissa asks, a little too calmly for Jason's taste. He studies her before he responds.

"I didn't have a plan if I am being honest. I was just going to come over, hope you would at least see me, and then figure it out from there."

"I guess that part was the figuring out?" Marissa asked.

"Look, Marissa. I really lov…I really like you a lot. I would like to get to know you and Jasmine…and I understand if you and I getting to know each other is not what you want, but please, at least give me a chance to get to know my dau…Jasmine," he pleads with Marissa.

"So Savannah is your niece, uh?"

"Yes, she is my niece."

"So is there any other leggy blonde or otherwise lurking around that is not your niece?" Marissa asks jokingly, yet Jason senses the seriousness in her question.

"There is no other. Someone already captured my eyes, a few years ago, one rainy night," he says, holding her gaze.

Underneath his gaze, Marissa again feels bare. She could feel the layers of her heart giving way. If she were being honest, her heart gave way the moment she opened the door. "So you are a ham and pineapple man, uh?"

Jason is confused, but he quickly gathers himself, "Yes, yes, ham, pineapple, umm…yes, ham and pineapple, yes I am." He grins nervously. Marissa giggles at how flustered he appears.

"Do you want to join us for a slice?" Marissa asks. By this time, Jasmine is back at the door, tugging on her mother's dress for her pizza. Marissa holds the door open and Jason steps inside. In his heart he silently whispers a prayer of thanks. *Colonel, I owe you one.*

Jason is grateful to not only be sitting there with Marissa, watching how attentive she is with Jasmine, but also, being in the same room with his daughter and the mother of his child is something he has dreamed of for a very long time.

Jason doesn't want to get ahead of himself, but he really likes this and could get used to being with them like this for the rest of his life.

Meanwhile, Marissa watches him from the corner of her eyes. He seems to be enjoying their company, and he is really good with Jas, and she has taken to him as well.

For a few seconds, Marissa fantasizes about what it would be like if they were living together like a family. Marissa quickly dismisses the thought from her head. She dares not hope to have found true love, not once, but twice.

***

Six months have passed since Jason showed up at her door after the concert. She has seen him several times since then when he comes to pick up Jasmine.

They have settled into a routine and have had picnics in the park and fun days at the beach as he gets to know Jasmine. She is grateful that Jasmine and Jason have developed a bond.

Watching the two of them play together warms her heart. It's evident that Jason is smitten with his daughter, and she too is smitten with him.

This day, however, is different, Marissa is going on a date with Jason, no babies allowed. She stares at herself in the mirror. Her hand touches the locket around her neck.

Behind her, Jade and Natalia walk in. Marissa looks up and smiles at them. "I'm gonna relieve you both of those keys soon if y'all don't knock before entering," she jokes.

Marissa has moved to a smaller three-bedroom home, closer to her parents' house. Graham and Nathan made sure they had everything for Marissa's and Jasmine's comfort. She had been blessed with two incredible fathers, always there for her without hesitation.

"You look gorgeous, Sissy," Jade says, kissing her. "Country boy will be writing another song about you when he sees you tonight."

"He won't have time to write," Natalia teases. "He'll be too caught up in all of this fabulousness." Marissa blushes bright red, and Jade and Natalia laugh.

"Is the dress too much?" Marissa asks, turning around, looking at herself in the mirror.

"Relax, Sissy, the dress fits you in all the right places. Trust me. He won't be able to keep his eyes off you," Jade reassures her.

"But do I want that though?" Marissa asked.

"Yes!" Natalia says. "You don't want him to take his eyes or hands off you."

"I don't know what you and Jackson have been doing, but you are this whole new wild person." She laughs.

Marissa gives herself another quick once-over as the doorbell rings. She takes up her keys and starts to head out. "Thanks for watching Jas, guys. Jae, please let her sleep."

"Why does she always assume I am the naughty aunt?" Jade asks Natalia.

"Because you are," Marissa says. "Don't wait up ladies." Marissa exits to girly giggles and screams.

***

Outside the house, Jason is standing with the car door open. This time he is clad in jeans, loafers, and a dress shirt. Marissa takes a deep composing breath before she walks toward him.

She awkwardly kisses him on the cheek when she reaches the car door, taking Jason completely by surprise. He clears his throat before hoarsely whispering, "You look amazing."

Score, Marissa thinks. *Now keep him off his game and all will be well.* Jason enters the car. He smells delicious. Marissa makes a mental note that she must figure out what cologne he wears. Whatever it is, it is downright amazing. He turns and looks at her, and Marissa feels instant chills.

"Are you warm enough; do you want me to turn down the AC?" he asks, flashing a smile.

Now it is Marissa's turn to be rattled. Her voice cracks as she answers, "Yes, I'm warm enough."

Jason pulls out of the driveway. On the radio some female singer is on, but Marissa's brain can't register what she is singing as Jason sits across from her. Somehow, the excitement in the air feels like it did the first night they met.

Jason glances across at her and wonders what she is thinking about. He wants to pull the car over and kiss her until her lips are swollen.

Her perfume fills his nostrils. It was the way his sheet smelled that morning after they first met when he woke up and she was gone.

Jason reaches over and holds her hand, bringing it to his lips to reassure himself that she is actually here with him. She shudders as his lips kiss her inner wrist. He is glad that he is affecting her as much as she is him.

The car pulls into the parking lot of the restaurant, and Jason turns the car off. He looks across at her. Even in the dimly lit car, her freckles are evident.

No longer able to help himself, he reaches over and pulls her to him and kisses her deeply. His kiss is familiar as his tongue pries her lips apart, seeking, demanding, tempting, tasting. Marissa moans as his chest presses up against hers.

He drops her seat back and fits her more comfortably into his embrace. His hands are on her shoulders, on the strap of her dress. He kisses a path down to her neck then back up to her cheeks.

Marissa has dreamt of this moment many times. She yearns for his touch. Her fingers are on the buttons of Jason's shirt, and she works them free, never breaking their kiss.

When her hands touch his chest, Jason pulls away. His reaction takes Marissa by surprise. She knows he wants her; it's evident in his eyes.

Jason takes her hand from his chest and brings it to his lips. He kisses each finger, paying special attention to every last one. His eyes never leave Marissa's. "I want you," he says. "And your body tells me you want me too." Marissa smiles up at him. He kisses a path from her fingers to her inner wrist. "But I cannot and will not have you until the day you decide to be my wife." His tongue traces circles on Marissa's wrist.

Her shocked expression makes Jason sit upright.

I'm pretty sure he just proposed to me. She looks at Jason. Her mouth opens and then closes as she does not know exactly what to say.

"Marissa, I love you. I really do. I have never stopped loving you. These past couple months with you and Jasmine, I have tried on several occasions to tell you this, but it never seemed like the right moment. This moment right now feels right...and I know it may be too soon for you to love me..."

Marissa cuts him off, "I've loved you too, Jason, since that first night we met. I still do." She reaches over and kisses him.

"Then marry me, Marissa. Let me love you forever," he says, holding her face. "Marry me. You and Jasmine are all I want in this world." He reaches over and fumbles in the glove compartment and pulls out a box. He opens it. Marissa stares at the ring inside

She remembers Stephen's words in the letter to her when she found the lockets, that she will know when to add to them. She looks at Jason, who is looking anxious and boyish like a nervous prom date.

He asks her again, "Marry me, Marissa." Her hand goes to the locket around her neck. She smiles at him.

"I'll marry you on one condition," she says, smiling broadly at him.

"Anything," Jason says, "just tell me and it is done."

"I need two photos of you," Marissa says, grinning.

Jason looks at her, puzzled. "Photos?" Jason laughs. "Marissa, I am asking you to marry me, and you're asking me about photos?"

Marissa reaches over and kisses him slowly, his lips, his jawline, his neck. "So am I getting those photos?" she asks between tiny kisses.

"Yes!" Jason says, dropping her seat all the way back, "Yes. What else do you want?" he asks as she kisses a path down his chest.

"You, but apparently I have to wait until our wedding night," she says, kissing him. He stares at her, demanding an answer.

"Yes, I will marry you." Jason's lips are urgent on hers. Marissa moans in pleasure. Jason's eyes are on fire as she looks up at him. He pulls away, knowing if he continues, he will not be able to stop himself.

"Why do you need the photos?" he asks her, curious. Marissa opens the locket now lying between her breasts.

"The letter that Stephen gave you pointed me to two lockets, this one and the one Jasmine wears around her neck." Jason studies the photo of his daughter inside. He is still puzzled.

"Stephen's note says that I will know when to add to them. Inside Jasmine's is a picture of me, and the other side is blank just like mine. My inscription says, *Whisper in the Night*, and hers says *Summer Sun*." Jason falls back in his seat, and his brain finally catches up.

"That's from my song." Tears wells up in his eyes, and he fights to hold them back. "He wanted you to add me to the lockets. Even to his grave, Colonel Paisley is still sacrificing for me."

He drops his seat all the way back and looks up at the stars through his sunroof. He reaches over and brings Marissa's hand to his lips. Marissa smiles at him. "This...us…, this, I believe, is the grace, Sharon…, my mom, speaks of."

Jason smiles at her, kissing her hand again. "Then it's that grace that saved me and led me to you." He whispers up at the stars, "Thank you for my family, Colonel."

Marissa holds the locket in her hand. She smiles at Jason then up to the stars. Even from beyond, Stephen is still taking care of her. In her thoughts, she hears him whisper, *Issa, you're my whole heart.*

***

Chapter 13

Marissa feels like sixteen again when she was preparing for the prom with Cameron. He was the star of the football team and the hottest boy in high school, and he wanted to go to the prom with Marissa.

Today however is her wedding day, and she is about to walk down the aisle to marry country music hottie Jason Edward Saunders. Marissa knows that she has been blessed to have found two great loves, first Stephen and now Jason.

In that moment she thinks of Stephen and wonders if he is looking down and is happy for her. She smiles at the thought, her fingers idly caressing the locket around her neck.

Jade and Natalia help put the veil on her head. She can hear their chatter, but she is lost in her own thoughts.

She is nervous. Her palms are sweaty, and she feels like she can't breathe, but it is a nervous kind of excitement. She has found love again, and it is with Jason.

She thinks about her conversation with him the night before when he snuck into her hotel room to steal a few kisses, and how he looked the night when he proposed to her.

She is filled with excitement and new hope for this new season, this new chance at love that God has granted her.

A knock at the door brings her back to the present as her mom's head pops through the door. "Hey, honeycakes, let me see my baby." Her mom has not called her baby in so many years, much less honeycakes.

She realizes that Stephen's passing has brought them closer together. Her mom became a tower of strength during the time she grieved Stephen and a wise counsel as she worked out her feelings for Jason, dealing with the guilt that she felt finding love or feeling love so soon after Stephen.

Sharon eyes Marissa. "I brought you something special," she says, kissing her daughter's cheek. Like an overly excited teenage girl, Marissa is anxious to see what her mom has hidden behind her back.

Sharon opens a tiny blue velvet box, and Marissa sees the most beautiful pair of earrings that she has ever laid eyes on. Marissa gasps.

Sharon says to Marissa, "These were my mom's and her mom's before her. They both wore them on their wedding day. I wore them on my wedding day. I was so upset with you at your last wedding that I failed to do my job as a mother and did not give you these earrings. I apologize for that."

"Oh, Mom," Marissa says, holding back tears.

"Mom, listen. You can't mess with her makeup right now," says Jade sternly, wagging her finger at her mom. "No, we're not doing the crying right now." Jade is already sobbing.

"You're messing up your makeup," say Marissa and Natalia together, half crying, half laughing. Natalia starts dabbing at the tears at Marissa's eyes.

Sharon says, "Can you forgive me, honeycakes?"

"There's nothing to forgive," Marissa says as she gets up and hugs her mom. "I love you. I am really glad you are my mom." Marissa and Sharon hug until Jade finally pulls them apart.

Sharon gives Marissa the earrings. She slips them in. "You're beautiful. You are beautiful. You are so beautiful," Sharon says to her daughter over and over again. "You look so much like your dad. I see him at times in your eyes, in your smile. You look beautiful." Marissa hugs her mom tightly, once again.

"Mom!" warns Jade again. "Come on. You're not being fair. You're not being fair right now. We can't do this today. She needs to look perfect. We can't have her walking down the aisles all puffy eyed and swollen face and nose. We don't want Jason to run when he sees her coming."

Sharon laughs at her youngest daughter as she shoos her out. "Go. Go. We're coming out." Sharon exits. "Let Dad knows we're ready!" Jade calls after her mother.

The next knock on the door is her father. The tears are already rolling from the time Graham walks in the room.

"Oh, Lord," says Jade. "We might as well ask Mom to come back in because this crybaby is going to be bawling all the way down the aisle. Maybe you should have asked Nathan to walk you down the aisle because at least I know you'd get down there. This one will not make it down because he's going to be sobbing all over the place."

Marissa laughs at her sister as her father is helplessly crying.

"You look so beautiful, Freckles. You are gorgeous," says Graham. Marissa kisses her dad's cheek.

"Are you going to be able to pull yourself together so we can do this?" Marissa asks, laughing at her dad.

"Yes, I can." He smiles at his daughter as he dries his tears.

Inside the church sanctuary, Jasmine walks down the aisles. Sharon walks alongside her as she drops tiny rose petals on the floor. Then Jade follows along with Jason's sister, Tamar, and his niece, Savannah, as they walk down the aisle.

Marissa appears at the door, her arms in her dad's hand. He is dabbing away tears. Jason looks down the aisle. Marissa is a vision, and his eyes drink it all in, almost like he is taking a mental image of this moment.

He silently thanks the Lord. He has no clue how he got this lucky, or rather, this blessed. He thought about Stephen and secretly thanks him in his heart.

The music starts playing, but Jason motions to them to stop playing. He has a special surprise for Marissa. As she walks down the aisle toward him, he takes the mic, and he starts to sing,

"I've searched the world to find you,

I've searched each stormy seas,

and there you were, silhouetted serenely,

under starlit heavens, robed in crystal raindrops, your heart calls out to me.

Here's my hand, together we will ride each crashing waves.

I won't let go; I am right here beside you. Together we will soar among the clouds.

Hearts entwined, we will rise… until our stories unfold among the stars..."

A smile stretches across Marissa's face. *Oh my good Lord. He is serenading me.*

Graham weeps even harder. "Dad, you gotta pull it together. We gotta make it down," Marissa says, laughing at her dad.

Marissa allows Jason's voice to wash over her as she walks down the aisle. She pauses at the section where she sees Cathryn and Nathan seated, their faces beaming. Marissa stops. She hugs them both. Nathan whispers to her, "You look beautiful, my daughter."

"Thank you, Dad," she says, kissing Nathan's cheek then Cathryn's while Cathryn wipes away tears.

She continues down the aisle to Jason as his voice beckons to her, pulling her closer. Jason ends the song as Marissa's dad stands before the pastor and hands Marissa's hand to him.

Graham says to Jason, "You have a gem here. Cherish her. Cherish them," he says, motioning to Jasmine. "Don't make me have to come looking for you, cowboy," he says.

Jason chuckles. "No, sir, you won't have to come look for me." Graham nods as Marissa laughs.

Marissa has never heard her dad act or talk all tough before and she chuckles even harder.

Jason takes her hand and brings it gently to his lips. "Hi, my darling. I see you made it here." He smiles down at her.

"Yes, I made it here," she says, looking lovingly up at him.

"Are you ready to get started with the rest of our life?" he asks. "Are you ready for this journey?"

Marissa smiles broadly at him. "As long as you're by my side, I'm ready to begin." Jason pulls her close to him. Lifting her veil, he plants a kiss on her lips. "We're not at this part yet," she says.

"I know." Jason grins at her with a charming smile, "Just a prelude of what's to come." Marissa tingles with excitement of the promise in Jason's voice and in his kiss.

His lips linger on her lips, both reluctant to pull away, as the pastor announces, "Let's begin."

****

The car pulls along the dirt road, pass the old, battered phone booth. The blue neon sign of HOTEL ATHENA inches closer as the car slowly navigates each pothole.

Marissa can't quite remember if there were so many potholes that night. She was too lost in the enthralling stranger sitting across from her. She pinches herself for a bit. She still cannot believe that a fated rainy night would lead her back here with the handsome stranger, Jason, now as her husband.

Jason looks across at her and smiles. She looks as ravishing as she did that night, except this time she is not soaking wet.

His hands reach over and takes hers and brings it to his lips. They are here, and this is all real. He smiles in amazement at how God works. He almost did not stop the night when he saw her walking in the rain. He was not in the habit of picking up strangers. But somehow, when he saw her drenched from head to toe, like a true damsel in distress, he had to rescue her.

In that one night, he found the love of his life and became father to the funniest, smartest, most amazing little girl in the entire world, his little Jasmine.

The car pulls into the hotel and the valet walks up and opens Jason's door. He motions to the other valet that is about to open Marissa's door that he has it. He steps out and makes his way around to her door and opens it. His tall muscular frame fills the doorway.

As Marissa exits, she presses up against him somewhat intentionally. "You're playing games, Mrs. Saunders," Jason whispers in her ears. His breath is hot on her cheeks.

"As are you, Mr. Saunders," she says teasingly. Reluctant to let each other go, they walk hand in hand into the hotel to check in. Jason ignores the familiar gawking of the associate as she checks them in. His eyes are only for Marissa and Marissa only.

As they enter the elevator, Jason pulls her in, completely ignoring the other patrons and kisses her passionately. Marissa giggles like a giddy schoolgirl as he nibbles at her ear.

Soon they were the only ones in the elevator and Marissa watches the numbers climb to the 12th floor as Jason kisses her throat and her shoulders. He swoops her up in his arms the minute the elevator doors opens and heads toward their room. He opens the door to room 1218. "You got the same room!" Marissa exclaimed in excitement.

Jason laughs at the surprise look on her face. "You're really trying to get me into your bed tonight, aren't you, Mr. Saunders?" Her arms around his neck, she kisses him.

"Oh, I fully intend to, Mrs. Saunders, he says grinning slyly. "And this time there's no escaping," he says, kissing her passionately.

Inside the room, the bed is covered with orchid petals. Jason gently lays her on them, her hair splayed around her shoulders. He looks down at her as she smiles invitingly up at him.

Her hand reaches for his, and he climbs on the bed beside her. Their kisses are hungry, yearning, longing as they work feverishly to remove the barriers that hold them captive from what they seek most, the touch of each other's skin.

Soon they are free and smooth silken skin glides against muscular hardness as they unite as one. He stares at her, his eyes ablaze with passion, her eyes are like shimmering ice on fire, and she can barely find words to express what she is feeling.

"Are you okay, my love?" Jason asks in a seductive tone.

"Yes" she whispers. "Yes, I am okay," she moans."

Together, they dance the ancient language of love. Marissa feels as if their stars have collided and broken into a million tiny little stars. Her mind is blank, thoughtless, free. She is completely caught up in the mastery that is Jason, from his kisses, his touch, to the way he slowly glides against her, as if savoring every move.

Final she gives in and completely lets go and Jason swiftly follows behind. She hears his satisfied growl as he shudders uncontrollably.

They lay there spent. Jason kisses her shoulder, then her neck, then up to her lips. She snuggles into him and drifts off to sleep.

Jason watches her, almost afraid to move. She is soft, angelic, perfect. How blessed he is to have found her. If he could frame a photo of time, it would be this moment. She has never been more beautiful, more alluring than she is right now.

He trails a path of tiny kisses along her cheeks, her lips, her neck, and as she snuggles in even closer, he too drifts off to sleep.

***

As the sun streams through the window curtains Jason stirs as a whiff of morning breeze hits his naked body. His eyes adjust to the sunlight streaming through, signaling the new day.

He reaches for Marissa, but she is not beside him. His heart races. For a split second, his mind went back to the day he woke up and she was gone.

Panic then fear sets in. His heart is racing faster, and he looks around for a note. He sees none. He fully sits up in bed and reaches for the phone.

Then she emerges from the bathroom, wet and ravishing, wrapped only in a towel. Jason's heart slows. "Are you calling down for breakfast?" Marissa asks.

"You're my breakfast," he teases, pulling her down on his lap while quickly masking his fears. Marissa giggles as he kisses her. "Who needs food when I have you." Marissa squeals loudly as he yanks her towel off and tosses it across the room.

"Housekeeping may have just heard us." She laughs as he tickles and kisses her.

"They have a strict no disturb order. We have years of catching up to do."

"Is that so?" she teases as he pulls her into him. His response is a low growl as the onslaught of kisses continues.

Several hours later, after they have feasted over and over on each other. Jason rolls on his side to face her. He kisses every finger, each wrist, then the palms of her hands. He looks at her searchingly.

"I have a confession." He pauses as if to gather his thoughts. "Earlier when I woke and did not see you, I thought you left."

That takes Marissa by surprise. She sits up and looks at him, "You thought I left as in went down to get breakfast left? Or..."

"Left, left, as in FOREVER IN MY HEART. XOXO! MARISSA kinda left," Jason says before she finishes.

"Wow," is all Marissa could muster. She realizes how her action hurt Jason the morning after they met.

An apology she knows will sound insincere. Instead, she pulls him up to her. They sit facing each other. She takes his hand and rests it over her heart, and she takes hers and rest it over his heart.

She looks at him "I know we said our vows yesterday, but here is a new vow that I'll make in the place where it all started. Where we first fell in love. I, Marissa Elizabeth Saunders, do solemnly vow to be the home that you always come home to. To be the safe space that you can always run to. To give you of mysel completely and to trust you beyond a shadow of a doubt. To intercede to God on your behalf daily. To protect your heart like a most treasured possession. To be yours and only yours, and to love you daily like it's our last day on earth. I am here and I am yours solely. Like Ruth says in the Bible, where you go, I go, where you stay, I stay. Your people are now my people, and your God is my God."

She kisses him deeply. There is promise, security and reassurance in her kiss and Jason willing drinks from it.

He reluctantly pulls away from her and stares at her lovingly. She has given him so much, and his heart is full of the purest kind of love he has ever felt.

He in turn places her hand on his heart and his hand on hers. He looks deeply in her eyes as he begins to speak. "I, Jason Edward Saunders, do solemnly vow to give you space to blossom and grow. To protect your heart with everything in me. To be patient and understanding if you and Jasmine need to grieve. To have eyes for you and you only. To pray over you and Jasmine daily. To be your confidant, your lover, your friend. To love every freckled inch of you daily until eternity ends, and most importantly, to love you, my wife, my lover, my friend, as Christ loves the church and to love you as my own body as it says in Ephesians 5."

He kisses her as she had kissed him before, deep, promising, reassuring, inviting. Marissa returns his kiss eagerly, her heart unguarded as she receives that which is covenanted.

Beneath sheer white curtains dancing in the afternoon Caribbean breeze, Jason once again makes love to his wife; this time they slowly explore every inch of each other. Leaving nothing unspoken, nothing unsaid. Each kiss, each touch is an affirmation and testament of what is and what is to come as together they etch their love story among ethereal stars.

****

THE BEGINNING...

4 Love is patient, love is kind. It does not envy, it does not boast, it is not proud. 5 It does not dishonor others, it is not self-seeking, it is not easily angered, it keeps no record of wrongs. 6 Love does not delight in evil but rejoices with the truth. 7 It always protects, always trusts, always hopes, always perseveres.
8 Love never fails…

1 Corinthians 13:4-8 NIV

COMING SOON FROM S.S. MCLEISH

NEXT IN THE *TANGLED HEARTS* TRILOGY: *SUMMER SUN*

Jasmine is a spunky twenty-one-year-old who lives in the shadows of her famous father, overprotective mother, and meddling grandparents. When Jake, the boy from the other side of the tracks, asks her to marry him, Jasmine must convince her family that he is the one for her.

***

Follow @ssmcleish on

www.ssmcleish.com

***

Download the single *Deja` Vu* on any music platform.
Artist: Maurice Gregory
Producer: Maurice Gregory
Songwriter: Shereece McLeish

www.ingramcontent.com/pod-product-compliance
Lightning Source LLC
Chambersburg PA
CBHW020516120726

47904CB00003B/850